THAT SUMMER

by H.M. Shander

Deborah,
Readers Rock!
Hope you enjoy;
♡ hm shander

That Summer
Published by H.M. Shander at CreateSpace
Copyright 2017 H.M. Shander

Cover Design: Melissa Gill of MG Book Covers & Design
Editing by: PWA & Natasha Raulerson Editorial
Shander, H.M., 1975—That Summer
ISBN: 978-0-9938834-6-0

First Edition
Printed by CreateSpace

Dedicated to all who ever hope
that when love finds them,
they are strong enough to face up to it,
and fall without abandon.
HMS

Table of Contents

❤ Chapter One ❤

"Again."

"No!"

"Yes. Dammit, we're going to try this again." She smacked her hand against the roof of the car for effect.

"Aurora…" Lucas said as he walked around and stood in front of her. "It's finished for tonight." Gentle, soothing hands gripped her shoulders as his reddish-blond head tilted down, his hair teasing the edges of his dark eyebrows. "And that's okay. We can try again tomorrow."

The parking lot was half-full of tenant vehicles, but the spots around Lucas' car were empty. It was the perfect location to play 'touch-the-car', and endeavor to sit in it. Tonight, she had tried. Multiple times. And failed miserably. The first shot at it, she could sit and touch the seatbelt, but with each successive endeavor, she worsened. Her last attempt to sit in the car, she launched back out as soon as her butt hit the seat. It didn't matter how many times she tried, staying any longer than a few seconds caused instant panic. At least she'd stopped puking. PTSD was a complete bitch.

Her gaze cast toward the other vehicles around them. Anywhere but him. Shame and hatred blanketed her—shame that she couldn't physically handle anymore, and hatred because of what she was trying to overcome. Normal people didn't need to fight post-traumatic stress disorder. Normal people didn't worry about their next car ride leading them straight to death. There was more hate than shame lately, which in itself was a good thing. It gave her something to fight against.

"Again, please Lucas." Her voice almost a whine. "Just one more time."

The tall man stood strong before her, his stance unchanging. "As much as I'd like to see you conquer this tonight, it's not gonna happen. You've pushed yourself all day. You're on the edge of falling apart." He flicked his hair away from his grey-blue eyes as they settled over her.

"But I can do it. I just need another…"

I can do this. I know I can. I just need another shot.

He shifted and closed the gap between them. "Your body and your mind need a break, okay?" When she didn't respond, he squeezed again. "Okay? Look at me." His hands smoothed out the wrinkles of her sleeves.

His soothing touch grounded her. When she flew off the handle, swore like a sailor, and lost all control, his gentle stroke from her shoulders to her fingertips brought her back to her senses. She couldn't explain the way it instantly calmed her racing heart, steadied her breathing, and focused her. Only that it worked. Every. Damn. Time.

She was so lonely and her body craved human contact. Since she'd quit her drug addiction cold turkey, all chemical relaxers were completely out of the question. Touch had become her drug of choice. She was allowed two Xanax weekly, and she saved them for those times where she was so overwhelmed she couldn't think straight. This wasn't one of them. She needed his comfort more.

She and Lucas had been working on Operation Save Nate for the past few weeks. Every day two steps forward, one and a half steps back. It was maddening. She was never going to conquer her fears in time.

Lucas tipped up her chin and said, "Take a deep breath."

Cool night air rushed into her lungs.

"Hold it for one… two… three… exhale." Long fingers tapped out the count on her shoulder, ending with a tender squeeze.

His gaze held hers as she released the air. "Thank you," she said.

"You're welcome."

Her shoulders sagged as she leaned against the car defeated. "Now what?"

"Tonight, we pack it in." The passenger door latched. "Tomorrow's a new day."

Her voice dropped. "Yeah."

He draped an arm across her shoulders. She leaned into him as they headed into the apartment building. Punching the correct floor, the elevator doors rolled shut in front of them.

"And what, may I ask, is on the docket for you tomorrow?"

Aurora faced him. "Work and back-to-back therapy appointments. Physio at three, shrink at four."

"With Chris?"

Chris Johnson was Lucas' older sister; a highly skilled psychologist working on her master's degree, and Aurora's mental health specialist. Or was.

"No, Chris thinks it's best to sever my dependency on her. Claims it's a conflict of interest or something because you're helping me win back Nate, so she keeps referring me out to other shrinks in her office." A small, awkward laugh escaped her lips. "But I haven't found anyone there yet that I'm comfortable with. We're running out of staff. I think there's one or two left, if the one tomorrow isn't right."

"You'll find someone."

"And if I don't?"

"There are others. Chris will find you someone awesome. She wants to help you just as much as I do."

And as much as Nate did. A long, low exhale. With it came another squeeze on her arm.

He pulled her closer. "I know that sigh."

"I know you do." She turned her body toward him. "Can I ask?"

"You can, but you know I won't tell you anything."

"But…"

"He's my brother."

The elevator dinged announcing her floor, and he held the door as she stepped through into the darkened corridor. The dingy carpet softened their footsteps as they walked the length of the hall.

"I just figured, being my best friend and all, that you'd–"

"I'm your best friend?" A playful smile erupted on his face, lighting him up.

She pushed him further down the hall. "Shut up. You know that."

He gave a low, throaty chuckle. "Yes, I do and I promise I won't tell Kaitlyn." Even in the lull of the dim light, his grey-blues sparkled.

Kaitlyn. Her cheerleader, former roommate and female bestie who was expected back from a month-long Russian holiday in the next forty-eight hours. A smile instinctively tickled the corners of her mouth as she yearned to catch up with her and show her how hard she'd worked to overcome her car phobia. She'd be a great trial. If Kaitlyn was impressed, Nate was sure to have his socks blown off.

Her heart ached. For Nate. God, how she wanted Nate to be the one standing in the hall with her now. Wanted his chocolate-coloured eyes on her, his lop-sided, one-dimpled smile lighting the area. Wanted to run her fingers through his ridiculously soft brown hair, but she'd screwed up. Not only had she screwed up, she'd also told him about it. Maybe at the time she thought she was doing him a favor or maybe she was sabotaging herself. Either way, he'd walked out, and her heart had shattered to pieces at the same time. But she knew, via Lucas, that Nate still loved her. In fact, he loved her so much despite her major screw up, he was preparing for his final race. He planned on retiring from his first love in nine weeks so the racing and car issues she had wouldn't be a problem between them. She didn't like that—not at all—and a plan to foil his career ending move was born.

Nine weeks. Sixty-three days to stop his retirement. The only way she figured she could succeed would be to show up at the track. It would prove she could handle his lifestyle, even if her PTSD from her automobile accident fought against that. In order to do that, she needed to get over her fear of touching cars, of sitting in them, of being strapped to them while they transported her around. It was the last one holding her back the most, but at the same time, she knew she was close to having a breakthrough on. Oh so close.

After unlocking the door, her coat puddled on the floor while Lucas walked straight into the galley-style kitchen and poured himself a glass of water.

She flopped into a cushiony kitchen chair. Watching him make himself at home amused her. It was inevitable, being that he was always

4

over. Always helping her. Always avoiding his family's questions about his whereabouts. Surely they didn't think he worked *that* much.

"Lucas, I can make you a tea or something."

"Nah, this is fine." The water went down quickly, and he refilled his glass. "Do you want me to make you one?"

"No." The chair wasn't where she wanted to be. She dragged herself onto her weathered old couch and sank into it.

The apartment wasn't much to admire, with its beige walls and dark-brown shag carpeting direct from the 1980s, but it was home. Carmen's paintings hung on every wall, adding a sense of cheer, although the canvases themselves were dark in colour. It comforted her to have her sister's presence in the room. Where paintings were on display, personal photos were in short supply. Only two were visible in the living room. One—a family photo before the crash—sat on an end table. The other picture hung above the flat screen TV console where her DVDs and gaming systems sat. An 8x10 photo of her and Nate taken on her first trip to the track. That was a day she'd never forget. The day she discovered he was a race car driver.

Lucas sat beside her after a few minutes, wiping his lips with the back of his hand. "You'll get through this, and you'll see him soon." He tipped his head in the direction of the photo she stared at constantly.

"How can you be so confident?"

"Because it's you. You're so determined to beat this that you will."

A sigh escaped her lips. She didn't bother suppressing it. "Doesn't feel like it."

"I know." He rubbed his brow. "Believe me, I know."

She pulled her leg under her and turned toward him. "That statement doesn't sound very positive."

"Sorry." The tight, pinched up expression on his eighteen-year-old face softened. "You've come so far. Remember how terrifying it was to just stand beside the open door? And then get in? Good lord, that was a fun time."

No need to remind her of it. Just thinking about it caused the hairs to stand on the back of her neck. It had been a scary day the first time they'd tried that. A shudder coursed through her as the memory flitted by.

She shook it away. "Can you tell me something about him? What's he been up to?"

"Well…" A sigh. "He's not the same without you."

"Yeah?" Her heart sped up every time Lucas said that.

Maybe it was what he knew she wanted to hear. Regardless, it made her feel good inside to hear it. Gave her more of a goal. More of a focus.

"You know this."

"Maybe, but I still like hearing it."

"You're hopeless, you know." He winked. "Anyways, he had a solid race yesterday. Came in third. He's doing well in the points standings. Second for now."

Shifting quickly, she pulled her legs to her chest, wrapped her arms around them and tightened. "I already know that. Tell me something new."

He smiled at her, and a flicker she'd never saw before appeared briefly when he spoke. "I'm not telling you anything more. You two will have to work that out when you get back together."

"If he'll take me back."

His eyebrow went up. "C'mon. You know better than that. He's gonna give up racing for you. Or at least he thinks he's gonna give it up." A snicker escaped him and he twisted in his seat. "I never asked because it's none of my business, but I am curious about why you broke up." He searched her eyes, and she broke the contact when she found her hands more interesting to stare at. "You don't need to tell me. I was just throwing it out there."

Shame held Aurora back. "What did he tell you? Maybe I can fill in the blanks."

It was a stretch, even for her, to hope Nate said nothing about Matthew—the insult to injury and the final shove to get him to walk away—but she knew better. Brothers share like sisters do, right?

Did Lucas know the truth?

As she stared at him, she studied his face. Hidden behind those eyes were a myriad of secrets and stories, but they never revealed a thing. It drove her crazy. She hated being the easy to read one.

Lucas shrugged. "Said it was the racing." He scrunched his brows and raked his fingers through his hair. "But it's more than that, isn't it?"

A slight nod. "I needed to push him away because I thought I couldn't handle being with someone who races car, especially when I couldn't even look at one. I needed him to walk away and never turn back. To find someone better. I'd hoped he come back begging, but he didn't. And why would he? I don't blend seamlessly into his life. But then you showed up announcing his retirement plans. I can't let it happen, right? I love him so much, so I need to win him back before he gives up the racing. I'm the one that needs to go crawling back on my hands and knees, not the other way around. However, I'm sure, if he'll take me back, every race will still cause me massive anxiety, but I'm willing to fight that to be with him. Does that make sense?"

"A little. I think it also jumpstarted something more. A desire to stop being a slave to your fears for starters. And that little drug problem. You're kinda kicking that to the curb as well."

"I suppose I am." A proud smile tickled at the edges of her mouth. "It was part of the problem."

He shifted beside her. "Well, it was and wasn't for Nate. He understood *why* you needed the Percocets and Xanax, he just didn't like how often you were using."

The withdrawal had been a living nightmare, but with the fog lifted from her mind, she had a clearer outlook on life. Not necessarily a happier one, but for once in a long time, she had a goal. That was a start. "Fair enough. Does he know I'm trying to stay clean?"

"How would I know?" A broad grin pushed against his cheeks, causing the corners of his eyes to lift slightly. "As far as Nate's considered, I don't know you."

Right. Another sigh. Of course Nate wouldn't know. Lucas was akin to a ninja therapist. No one knew, aside from his sister, where he spent his time, and he kept mum with everything said between them. Especially the things flying out of her mouth in the heat of the moment.

Too many times she wondered about the predicament she put him in. He was loyal to both his brother and her. When the summer was all said and done, she figured Lucas would end up needing therapy too.

❤ Chapter Two ❤

Lucas slammed the door to the apartment, making her jump. The butter knife flew out of her hand and clanged as it landed in the sink. An hour ago, he texted he had finished at the track for the weekend and was on his way over. As was usual he came in time for Sunday Sandwiches. She made his favourite—peanut butter, honey and banana.

Cheeks red with anger, he asked, "What the hell happened Friday?"

A blank look registered on her face. *Where had that come from?*

"All week long, we've been good, right? I work, have supper with the fam, and then I'm here." Pacing back and forth in the eating area, he rambled on. "On Thursday evening, everything was hunky-dory. Nate even told me–" He shook his head, strawberry-blond hairs flying in every direction. "It doesn't matter what he told me." A spin in his step, he turned to confront her. "*Something* happened on Friday. *Something* caused him so much pain because his recent behaviour is so not Nate. I don't want to pry, dammit, but if you and I are gonna work, there can't be secrets between us." He stomped closer to her, his finger waving furiously between them.

Track rules, right? No secrets. Otherwise the team as a whole can't function.

His arms crossed over his chest, his jaw clenched tight. "Want to explain to me why he's seeing Marissa?"

"What?" The surrounding air turned icy. She struggled to breathe. "Marissa Montgomery?" The name rolled off her tongue like a bad disease.

"Yeah. I'd love to know why that hoe-bag had her mitts all over Nate."

She breathed in a cool breath. "Marissa, the two times I've seen her, she had no issue openly flirting with Nate in front of me."

Lucas paced around the living room and into the eating area, stopping for a moment. "Yeah, but it was never like this. And Nate, dammit, he usually resists, but–" A violent shudder shook Lucas. "Eww." His hands covered his face, and he slowly pulled them down, making his eyes wide and wild. "So, seeing them together…" He made a retching motion. "… Led me to believe that they are together. So… What the hell happened Friday? Because on Thursday he was talking about a future with you."

Unable to stand properly, she braced herself against the wall. No, it wasn't strong enough. Her jelly-filled legs refused to support her, she needed a seat. Stumbling over to the couch, she slumped into it and grabbed the nearby blanket to cover up. It didn't matter if it was 29C outside. The air in the apartment chilled her to her bones.

"You need to tell me. There's some sick reason he's with her, and I'd like to get to the bottom of it."

In a low whisper, fighting to breathe, she said, "Ask him."

Oh my god. It's over. The training, the learning, to trying to win him back. It's gone. He's with someone else.

Her body shivered as her heart slid into her stomach.

"I did." Lucas walked over and sat beside her on the couch. He lowered his voice. "He told me to ask you."

"Oh."

Is he with Marissa because of me? How much did Nate see on Friday?

The colour drained from her face as it replayed in her mind. Hope blossomed for a fraction of a second.

Maybe that's not why. Maybe it was something else.

Her head snapped to stare at him. "Does he know?"

"About what?"

"You being here. Us working together?"

Oh god. What if Nate thinks Lucas and I are a couple?

"I don't think so."

Hmm... weird.

Unable to shake off the uneasiness, she asked in a hushed tone, "Then why would he tell you to ask me?"

"Geezus, Aurora. You're missing the point. He said *you're the reason* he's with Marissa. And the way he said it..." He shook his head. "What the hell happened? Was it at work?" The tone in his voice lowered to a more soothing, less accusatory level. "Did you two have a fight? Dammit, I shouldn't have ignored my nagging feeling to show up at the library that afternoon, but I didn't want it to look suspicious."

Friday. Nate's angry because of what he thought he saw on Friday.

"If I tell you, you'll hate me just as much as he apparently does."

"He doesn't hate you." Lucas rubbed her leg. "I know he doesn't. If he did, he wouldn't have been so quick to bring up your name. But he's angry. That's the only explanation for him being with her. Please, tell me what happened? Did something happen at work?"

Her head hung in shame as she sighed. "Fine." The blanket wrapped tighter around her. "But I'm letting you know first that I was a bad person. Really bad. It was mostly the drugs though because a sane and clean person wouldn't have done what I did."

"Why am I suddenly worried?"

She whispered, "Do you know who Matthew James is?"

"Yeah, of course." He nodded in confirmation. "He's that author guy."

"Well, he did a show at the library in May." Now it was her turn to shudder. What a jerk he was, and what a hoe-bag—is that what Lucas called Marissa?—she had been. "So, anyways, long story short, I met him. Matthew James, I mean. He asked me out, but I stood him up."

Lucas' expression morphed from amazement, to shock, and ended with a scowl. "Why?"

"Matthew made some rude comments behind my back."

"I see."

"Anyways. I got over it. However, because the universe doesn't already hate me enough, it turns out we're connected."

He pulled her legs across his, and using his powers of relaxation, rubbed her feet. "Remind me to make sure you bring that up in therapy. The world doesn't hate you."

"Do you want me to finish?"

"Fine." He leaned back and waved her on.

"So, this connection. Turns out Matthew's wife was in the car that hit and killed Momma and Carmen."

"No shit."

"Yeah. It gets better, in a sick kind of way." Another shudder coursed through her. She braced herself for what she had to say and it wasn't pretty. "So I agreed to meet up with him the next time he was in town as I wanted more information on it. He obviously knew more about the crash than I did. Nate and I had just broke up. Or at least I thought we had. Nate said we didn't. Which makes the next part even worse."

He grimaced, pushing harder into a tender spot on her foot.

"Ouch." She yanked her foot back, hurting her hip.

Dammit. And physio's a few days away. It's hard enough dealing with the hip pain without my Percs, but to be so stupid in yanking back my foot. Damn.

She rubbed her hip, ignoring the stare down from Lucas.

He glared at her. "Tell me you didn't?"

The hairs stood at attention on the back of her neck, and goosebumps pimpled her flesh. "Well, in my defence, my very *weak* defence, I was high. Very high. I fell that night and bruised my hip. I took a combo of Percs, Xanax and something else to feel numb. Like borderline hallucinogenic high."

"Aurora."

Ouch. That pity-filled tone stung. Her chin nearly touched her chest when she continued. "I thought Matthew was Nate when he kissed me. I honestly did. All I saw was Nate's face. Every touch I honestly believed was Nate's touch."

"That's disturbing." He shook his head and pulled back just enough to notice. "You were out of your mind."

"I really was. And the next morning, Matthew was still there. I immediately ended whatever it was *he* thought was going on. Then Nate and I got back together, and all was good. I never mentioned my mistake. However, Matthew wouldn't leave me alone. He texted me details about the trial, and as much as I wanted to let him go, I couldn't. It was because of Matthew that I understood what was going on with the trial. My own father wasn't as forthcoming with information."

His voice deepened as he leaned toward her. "That had to have been difficult."

"Thank you." A nod of understanding. "It was and still is. As terrible as Matthew was, he's also the link to a part of my past."

"Something you're not ready to let go of yet."

A small shake of her head. "Anyways, this past week, the sentencing was being deliberated, or whatever the hell they call it. Well... Friday afternoon Matthew came to the library to check on the final preparations on the new wing." She searched Lucas for understanding, hoping he'd show some kind—any kind of emotion. Instead, he was a blank slate. Something she envied. "And he came with news to deliver in person."

Lucas pulled himself closer, but retained his poker face.

"He told me about the sentencing. Thomas Anderson, the driver, is going to prison for a long time."

"That's great news." He reached out and touched her hand, rubbing her knuckles with his rough thumb.

She hadn't shared any of this with him before, and even as awful as it was, she felt a burden being lifted from her. Things didn't seem so terrible. But an image of what went down Friday afternoon flashed in her mind like a neon sigh. "Yes, it was a little overwhelming to hear it. I didn't realise Nate was in the staff room. I swear to God I didn't." She flicked away his hand and gripped the blanket tightly in her fists. "I started crying, right? This was the news I'd hoped for. A bit of closure in a way."

"Yes."

"Well, the jerk thought my tears meant something else, weakness or what, I'll never know." She swallowed and shuddered. "He kissed me."

"And you let him?" The disgusting tone in Lucas' voice was clear as a bell.

"No! Never."

"But Nate saw?"

"I assume as much, as he left in a huff. I slugged Matthew as hard as I could, screamed a string of profanities that would've embarrassed a trucker, and chased after Nate, but he peeled out of the parking lot when I got close. I tried texting him, but I got nothing."

"Oh, Aurora." His voice wavered, an undercurrent of disgust cutting through.

"I know. I hate myself too." If hatred were a pit, she'd be halfway to the other side of the world by now.

"So, he must've thought you were back dating Matthew?"

"I'd never told Nate it was Matthew I had my… indiscretion with. Nate knew I'd been with someone because I told him, but I never mentioned who it was."

"I'm sure he figured it out."

"Yeah," she said, her voice falling to the floor. "I'm sure he's put it all together by now." She leaned her head against the back of the couch. The room went silent aside from the occasional sigh. "So it's over for good now, isn't it?"

"What do you mean?"

"Well, he's with her. He won't leave Marissa for me. And why would he? She's beautiful. She's into race cars and has no fear of them. They have so much in common. She'd be able to convince him not to retire."

He sidled up closer to her. "Yeah, they have cars in common, but that's about it. Aside from that, I can't even figure out why they'd be together. He has much higher standards than that. She's a hoe-bag with a dirty reputation. Nate sticks with clean-cut, wholesome types."

She let out a loud laugh. "Then what the hell was he doing with me? I'm so far from clean-cut and wholesome."

"For now, but maybe it's there. You know? Hidden underneath this tough exterior you broadcast to the world." A tiny smile caused the corners of his mouth to turn up. A vast improvement over the so serious you've-screwed-everything-up-again expression. "Well, there had to be something about you he latched onto."

"Yeah, well the jury's still out on that one."

"If you say so." He winked. "Marissa though… she's just… well, she's not even a nice person. I'd hate for her to be my sister-in-law."

She whipped her head up at him so fast she kinked her neck. "What??" A putrid green filled her soul. And it wasn't from jealousy.

Lucas laughed while shaking his head. "Let me explain. Every person I know who dates someone, I question whether or not they'd be a great fit with our family. I get something like a sixth sense about these things. Like Chris and Max, he's perfect for our family, although he needs to hurry up and commit already. Balances with Chris quite nicely. Just like Bill does with Mom. But we'll see how that goes."

She was afraid to ask. "And... me?"

"Yeah, I thought about it."

She leaned forward to hear his response.

"It wouldn't have worked out."

"Oh," she said, slumping into the blanket. Unguarded, the tears fell fast and furious.

"Kidding," he said quickly.

She playfully punched him in the shoulder. It wasn't very hard, more like a tap. "You're a jerk."

"And you're finally seeing it." His infectious laugh filled the room as he pushed her back.

The tears damped her knees as she rested her heavy head.

"Well, now that I've trampled all over your emotions, what should we do today?"

She barely heard what he said as her heart sunk like a lead weight in her stomach. Lucas made a bad joke about things not working out between her and Nate but she couldn't shake the feeling he was on to something. How could she be part of a family when half of them didn't want her around? Lucas' mom had said it wasn't the best time for her to be involved as it ruined Nate's concentration and Chris was trying to distance herself. Poor Lucas. "What do they think you're doing all the time?"

"What? Who?"

"Your family. You're gone all day, and sometimes into the wee hours of the night. They must think you're up to something."

"Well, Chris knows what our plan is."

Lifting her head up, she leaned her chin onto her knees. "I know that. But Nate? And your mom? What do they think you're doing?"

Lucas practically lived in her apartment during the week, they had to have some concerns over it.

"All that matters is that I'm here to help you."

"Come on. Even Daddy questions the amount of time we're putting into this little project."

"Little project? Good lord, what do you consider a major one?" He huffed and let out a breath.

"No really, don't change the subject. Where do they think you are?"

He closed his eyes for a second as he rested his head on the back of the couch. "I'm having an issue, no actually, it's mom who's having the issue."

She reached for his hand as it tapped against her foot. "What's going on?"

"We're having some disagreements. On a few things. The most major one being university."

Pulling her legs off him, she sat upright and leaned into the couch. "What about?"

"I don't feel mechanical engineering is the best place for me anymore."

"So switch faculties."

"It's not that easy."

"Sure it is." Without missing a beat, she shrugged. "I did it."

"I have thousands of dollars in scholarships. All earmarked for Mech. There are no additional funds for me to go into something else."

Aurora wiggled in her seat, scooting closer to him. "What about taking a year off? Or a semester? That would give you time to save up."

"That would work if it wasn't for the fact I'd earned the Lester Johnson Scholarship."

"Was that named after your father?"

"Grandfather. Dad was the recipient and so was I. If I don't use it…" His head hung low.

"You'd be doing a disservice to your family." She rubbed his arm. "I get that. It's a tough place to be."

Lucas sighed and ran his fingers through his hair. "It is. And the fights. It's just easier to stay away." Strong hands twisted in his lap and he answered her question before she had a chance to formulate it.

"Things aren't so bad when we're out on the track. We have a million things to do, so there's no time to discuss the school situation."

"Have you talked to Nate?" She reached out and held his hand to stop his knuckle cracking. Nate was always the voice of reason, at least with her.

"Yeah, but he's not much help. He loves being in engineering so he doesn't understand why anyone would want to leave it."

"You're right, that's not much help." She sighed along with Lucas. "Well, we still have time to come up with a solution."

By the end of summer, she had planned to give him part of her earnings as a surprise, but she highly doubted there would be enough to cover tuition for a year, or even a term. Maybe she could ask her father, but that might be too much.

Oh Nate. If only you were here. We could sit and figure this out.

She could imagine snuggling into his chest, his arms wrapped around her tight. He'd have a faint smell of fresh air mixed in with the track scent of rubber and fuel. Ordinarily, it would be a turnoff, but with Nate, it just made him sexier. And thinking of his sexiness made heat pool in her core.

Stop. Stop. Forget about him right now. Focus on Lucas. Focus on finding a solution. He's been so focused on me and training.

The training nagged at her. Eventually this was going to work. It had to.? At some point in the near future she'd be able to get into a car. It had to happen. It was beyond disgusting to her how much of a hold the PTSD had over her, and how powerless she felt fighting it.

In the depths of her brain, a tingling formed. A feeling she couldn't shake. The need to move right now overwhelmed her. She flung the blanket to the side got up, storming into the kitchen. Working her jaw she stomped back to the living room. Her feet planted on the carpet, the tingling pressing before she grunted and returned to the kitchen.

"It's building again?" Lucas said from behind her.

She hadn't noticed him move. "Yep."

Like a bright neon-sign on a dark street, the word *failure* flashed in her brain. Over and over. It was just a word, and she tried to reason it was powerless, but it filled her with guilt. And shame. Copious amounts of shame.

"What's wrong?" he asked.

She slammed her eyes shut as she gripped the counter. "I don't know exactly."

A roving check over her body told her nothing was out of the ordinary. It wasn't an anxiety attack building, but something else. Her pulse wasn't racing, just beating faster. Her breathing was normal too, even with her pacing. If she could somehow make it to her bedroom undetected, there was a little packet of happiness waiting to calm her. She searched her brain trying to figure out how to get there without Lucas knowing.

He spun her around and held her shoulders with a firm grip. "Look at me."

She shook her head.

I don't need comfort. I need something chemical.

The pull toward it was overwhelming.

I just need one.

His voice penetrated her thoughts with his deep, throaty sound. "Aurora, look at me."

After a deep, three-count breath, she glanced around and focused directly on Lucas' unshaven jaw, the growing stubble more reddish than blond. His lips in dire need of Chapstick. A tiny pimple grew on his left cheek that she wanted to pop. She avoided eye contact. It's not what would calm her right now. There was something special for that, but it was hidden. If only.

"What are you thinking?" he asked.

I can't do this.

She stood there for a few breaths, wondering if she should take him to her bedroom or leave the apartment.

"Come with me." With a firm grip on his hand, she pulled him toward the bedroom.

❤ Chapter Three ❤

"Umm," he said, hesitating and protesting as she dragged him down the hall. "What's going on?"

Her head shook from side to side. "Whatever you're thinking, you're wrong."

They entered her bedroom. Nothing fancy; a dresser without a mirror, a queen-sized bed, and little book-sized tables on either side of the headboard. No TV, just a clock radio. The open brown curtains revealed a gorgeous summer day, betraying the dark grey storm brewing inside her mind.

They stopped at the foot of her bed. Unable to look at him, she dropped to her knees on the side closest to the window. She blew out a series of short breaths, hoping to gain control. It was failing.

Eyes closed, she thrust her hand between the mattresses and felt around, moving her hand left and right until she touched the plastic package with the foil wrapper. Pulling it tightly between her fingers, she slowly extracted her hand. Big, fat, guilt-heavy tears fell as a sob ebbed within her soul. The hand holding the pills shook like a leaf on a windy day.

As Lucas dropped down beside her, his colour faded fast.

Her hand moved towards him and opened to reveal a package of Benedryl pills. Half the blister packs opened.

"I'm sorry," she sobbed. "I... needed... something... Friday."

The package fell to the floor as Lucas pulled her into his arms.

"I'm... so... sorry."

Tears of regret, of shame—of hatred—funnelled out of her. They poured faster than ever, each wave threatening to rip her in half. "I'm not as strong as you think."

Lucas held her tight as she soaked his shirt with her guilt-filled sobs. Glued to him, her body racked with shame, he never let go. Time lost all meaning. If hours had passed, it had felt like mere minutes as the self-hating negative thoughts swirled in her head. If it had been minutes, her worn out body made her feel as if she'd been in his arms forever as her tears ran out.

The sound of an engine revving muffled from deep in his pocket, breaking their connection. "It's okay. It's Nate."

She pulled back and wiped her eyes. "You should get it."

"It's not important."

The sound continued.

"Please." She righted herself and moved back against the table.

Lucas yanked out his phone. "What's up? I'm in the middle of something *really* important right now…" He remained focused on her, an expression of confusion clouding his features as he spoke. "I'll get back to you and let you know… Not really… Unlikely… Fine, later." He hung up and tossed the phone to the bed. His mouth opened and shut again, and he shook his head.

The longer time stretched out, the thicker the silence grew.

In a voice she thought belonged to someone else, she asked, "Are you mad at me?"

"Umm, I don't know. No, I don't think so." The package flipped over in his hand. His voice broke when he asked, "Are there any more?"

She shook her head, hair whipping sharply against her chin. "No."

"Okay." He pushed it into his back pocket and stood, extending his hand for her. He pulled her to her feet and without warning, wrapped her in a hug. "Thank you," he whispered into her ear. "Thank you for trusting me with the truth."

She wasn't sure, but she wondered if he was crying. His body seemed stiff against hers, but his chest moved rapidly. Not wanting to ask, she wrapped her arms around him and tightened.

The embrace ended when he stepped back, not even trying to hide his red and glassy eyes.

What've I done to you? Her eyes darted between his. "I'm so—"

His finger covered her lips. "As am I. But…" He blinked rapidly and swiped his hands across his face. After a deep breath, he ran his hands through his hair. "Well… There's nothing else you're trying to hide from me?"

A weight had been lifted, and as awkward as the air was, at least she wasn't being held down by secrets. It was shame and hatred that kept her cemented to the ground.

"I finally got some sleep," she said in a weak laugh, trying to lighten the mood. It had been weeks since she'd had a solid sleep. Insomnia, a gift from the withdrawal Gods, had settled in for a long time.

"Not funny."

"Sorry."

"When did you take them last?"

"Friday night. I took four."

His eyes bugged out.

"Last night I took three."

He nodded slowly, casting his focus downward as his brows pulled in. "Okay." A quick tap-tap-tap of his lips before he spoke. "Since you were honest with me…"

She swallowed and sat beside him, hunching her shoulders as she pulled her legs close. A tingling in her chest radiated out to her limbs.

He talked in a low voice as if to only reach himself. "I need to tell someone about the pills, as this is bigger than you and me… but I don't know who we can trust. Chris? Maybe. I'm sure my sister would have all sorts of crazy ideas, maybe even a couple of good ones. Your dad? I really want to, and think he has a right to know, especially since he was here for the initial withdrawal. But I suspect he'd be quite upset and I don't know if that's what you need right now." A low groan escaped him. "I really don't know what to do with this." His finger tapped his lips in a constant flurry of motion as he sat beside her gazing off into the distance.

Her heart plummeted to her stomach where it flipped and soured. The warmth from her cheeks cooled in fear. It was hard to sit there listening to him babble on and see him so upset. All because of her. If she had just…

What? What could I have done Friday night that would make this better? I couldn't have, and wouldn't have called Lucas. I couldn't pull him away from the track. That's so unfair. And Kaitlyn, she worked Friday night and was going clubbing. I didn't want to be alone, and I didn't want to be with anyone. I'm such an idiot.

"Hey," Lucas said as if her thoughts registered on her face. "We'll get through this. I promise. Maybe I should stay here for a few days? Help you through this dark space you're in?" He reached for her hand and struggled to open it. "Jesus H. Christ, Aurora." His jaw dropped, and he ran his thumb over the crescent-shaped indents in her palm.

Her throat was too dry to speak.

I know.

A bubbling of manic energy built within her, sending her heart racing and increasing her respiration. "I need to get out of here."

I need to make this right.

"Do you want to go for a walk?"

She straightened up and stared at him. "No. Let's go for a drive."

"Are you sure you want to do this?"

"Unlock the damn door, Lucas." If she was calm and collected in the elevator ride down, she wasn't now. She shook beside the car while Lucas unlocked and held the door open for her.

"We're going to do this. Now." She placed her hands on the roof. "UB's Sports Pub is less than two minutes that way." Her finger pointed south.

"If you say so. You're the boss."

A couple of quick and very shallow breaths later, she sat in the passenger seat. Her eyes slammed shut.

You can do this.

No, you can't.

You're crazy. You're talking to yourself.

"Shut up," she said, as her mouth dried up.

See, nut job?

"I didn't say anything," Lucas said.

You can do this.

A few more breaths. Her heart would explode from her chest if it weren't for the ribcage enclosing it.

"All good?" he asked.

She couldn't move her head, and her lips were frozen shut. Slowly, with a shaking hand, she managed to give a thumbs up sign. She only hoped he could see it.

"Do you want me to buckle you in? Or do you want to do it?"

We can't move until it's done, but I don't know if I can handle being strapped in. Maybe I should've thought this through. I wanted to show him I'm not a complete shithead, but this is too much.

"Aurora, do you hear me?"

She gave a small nod. "It's cold in here."

"If you say so." His voice sounded as though he stood twenty-feet away from her.

It felt like she'd been transported to Hoth; everything around her was icy cold. With her eyes still closed, she felt behind her for the buckle.

I can do this.

Lucas' rough hands wrapped around hers. The cool metal was snug between them. Shaking violently, she pulled it across her body. A river of sweat trickled down her back, even though she was chilled to the bone.

"I'm still here," Lucas said.

She gave a small nod. The metal in her hands clinked against the arm rest on her left side. Her left hand danced around for the connector while her right gripped the main piece tightly.

"Just breathe. You want the clip in your right hand to slip into the buckle in your left hand."

How in the hell does he keep his voice so calm?

"That's it," he said. "Nice and slow. Take a deep breath."

Inhaling a large gulp of air, she steadied herself and breathed. Another tiny nod.

"You've got this." His voice came from in front of her. "Almost there."

The fingers of her right hand touched her left.

So close.

She held her breath as the metal pieces joined and clicked together. Tears built up behind her closed eyes.

I don't want us to crash. I don't want to watch it happen again. I don't want Death taking someone else I care about away.

"You did it." His voice oozed with pride.

She held back a scream, feeling her legs tighten with each breath.

I'm buckled in.

A hint of a weak smile forced its way through. It only came out for his behalf.

I'm buckled into a car. Oh. My. God. I'm buckled into a car.

Bile inched up her throat, tickling at the edges.

Not here. Not in his car.

She swallowed it down, panting as it slowly retreated. A warm hand touched her knee, and Lucas hunched over in front of her, popped into view.

"I'm right here," he said.

Air rushed in and out of her lungs faster than her racing heart.

"We're not going anywhere until you okay it." His voice was slow and even, calm and oddly comforting. "Alrighty? Can you speak?"

Her eyes darted between his and she went to open her mouth, but no sound came out.

"That's okay. Let's stick with the thumbs up sign." Lucas stood there patiently waiting for her to respond. "When you're ready, I'm gonna close the door," he said. "I'll just stay beside it until you give me the sign. Okay?"

Rivers of sweat merged on her back. Her arms shook from nervousness. Slowly, she remembered how to make the sign.

"Okay, great. I'm closing the door."

Her immediate world darkened as her eye lids shut. Goosebumps bubbled along her arms. It was so cold inside the car she wished she'd worn a sweater. The door shutting into place was too much.

"NO!" she said, finding her voice. A microsecond later, a breeze blew across her body as the door opened.

"It's all good. Door's open." His warm hand squeezed her shoulders. "I need you to look at me okay?"

She let out a heavy sigh, but listened to him all the same and opened her eyes.

"I'm right here." He squatted down beside her. "Maybe that's it for today? You've done so well. It's been a helluva day. We can attempt this another time."

Delicately, her head moved from side to side.

"Hmm... okay." He reached for her hand and ran his thumb over her knuckles. "How about I roll down the window first, before I close it?"

She couldn't move.

Cold air replaced his warmth as he stood. "I'm going over to my side now."

Turning her head, she followed him around the vehicle and watched as he slipped behind the wheel. Putting the key into the ignition, he twisted it just enough to power up the dash and roll the windows down. With a quick turn, he twisted the key back and pulled it most of the way out, leaving it dangling.

A second or two later, he was back at her side. "You hanging in there still?"

I think I can do this.

Breathe.

It's all good. We're safe. Car's not moving.

The thumbs up sign slowly took form in her right hand.

Lucas shut the passenger door, but never moved away.

In rapt fascination, she focused on his hands. They were much rougher and dirtier-looking than Nate's. His hands were soft.

A slow nod, and he sprinted around the driver side door, slipping once again behind the wheel. "All good?"

She inhaled a large amount of air.

I think so.

"Before I even start this up, I need some kind of sign. Words. Signal. A nod. Something."

Give me a minute.

She looked around. All was good. Totally safe. She was breathing. Seatbelt on. She was still alive. Lucas sat beside her. Death wasn't here, at least not that she could tell. However, she was still in the parking lot.

Damn.

She'd hoped she would've been transported to the pub magically. Turning her head gently to the left, she said. "Let's. Do. This."

"Alrighty."

Without taking her focus off him, the engine roared to life, and she instinctively gripped the arm rest with her right while her left flew frantically through the air.

A warm hand wrapped around it. "I've got you."

Her stomach flipped and her vision went blurry.

"Maybe we should try this another day?"

She shook her head. "Give me a minute." A slow breath did nothing to tame the wild acceleration of her heart. "Go."

"Go?" His grey-blues questioned and his head tipped.

"Yes." She let go of his hand as he moved it toward the shifter.

In a swift moment, she felt the rush of a backwards movement before the vehicle came to a stop. The shallow breathing made her lightheaded. Suddenly, without warning, she pushed back into the vinyl seat as Lucas put the car in gear and rolled forward.

"Umm... mmm...." She hummed as her hands squeezed together and turned them white. Over the driveway. Bump. Bump. Her grip tightened impossibly. "Umm... ummm... mmmmm..." Words failed to escape her but deep instinctive groans had no problem. Their pitch escalating with every passing second.

The car pulled up to the stop sign, and the blinker echoed through the tiny space. "Hang on," he said, inching the car out into the intersection.

"Ohmygod. Ohmygod," she repeated over and over as the car gained speed, and houses quickly disappeared from her peripheral vision. She closed off any further visualization. "No. No. No." A sour feeling filled her stomach. Air chilled in her lungs, making her gasp. "Nate," she whispered.

Out of the darkness, his face appeared in front of her. "You've got this," his voice said. "Just breathe. You're nearly there."

"Oh Nate." A warm hand covered hers.

"Breathe in and out."

She followed his instructions to the letter. Air in, air out. Again. Her focus on his chiselled jawline. Those chocolate-coloured eyes. That dimple in his cheek. Still, she knew where she was, but she also knew she wasn't alone. Tears she'd held back released, making hot rivers down her cheeks.

"Nearly there," Nate's soft voice whispered in her ear.

"I can't do this."

"But you *are* doing this. You're doing so great."

"Hold me. I'm scared."

"I can't." The voice faded away, and the image of him disappearing like a wave across the ocean.

The rivers ran harder down her cheeks, and as she tightened her grip, her nails dug into the souls of her hand. The pain was welcome. At least it was physical and she could make it stop in a heartbeat.

The car slowed and the engine died. Lucas unlatched her seatbelt. The door sprung open seconds later.

"You did it." His voice was warm and full of pride.

Slowly, she opened one eye, then another. They were in a parking lot. The neon sign read "UB's Pub and Eatery". She did it! And with that she popped out of her seat and into Lucas' arms.

"You did it," he said, excitement ringing through the air.

The sobs inside her burst forth, and she broke down in his embrace, collapsing to the asphalt.

"You're still alive. We didn't crash." His hands ran over her head and pulled her close. "Hey, hey, hey. It's okay."

Everything she'd held back, poured out in her tears. She clenched Lucas' soft-cotton shirt and buried her head into it. Body-wracking sobs consumed her for the second time that day, but his strong arms held her tight. With a sniff, she broke out of his hold.

"You okay now?"

She wiped her sleeve under her lashes and over her nose. "I think so."

"You really rocked that. You were amazing."

An older couple walked by staring intently at them as they huddled on the ground. She didn't care what they were thinking. They had no idea of the hell she'd just put herself through.

Lucas waved them away.

The sun beat down on her, slowly warming her up but the intensity threatened to blind her. Instinctively, she shielded her eyes from the bright light. "It felt like we were never going to arrive."

"First time will probably be the worst. Maybe, hopefully, each trip will be easier."

"No offense, but I'll be walking home."

He laughed at her statement. "Are you able to stand?"

Once standing, she dusted off her pants. "Sorry for that outburst."

"You have nothing to be sorry for. Besides, I wouldn't have expected any less. That was a huge step." He held open the door for her as they entered the pub. "Go clean yourself up and I'll get us a table."

Twangy, old-style country music floated over them from the speakers in the ceiling. The interior of the pub remarkably bright with a long wooden bar flanking the left side, and a variety of tall bar tables and chairs scattered across the floor. She made her way to the bathrooms. A distressed-looking divider separated the washrooms from the otherwise open and empty space.

A young waitress, sporting more fringe than was cool, passed by her and stopped instantly. "Hey, are you okay?"

"Yeah." She dug into her pocket and pulled out some cash. "This should more than cover whatever we order."

The waitress tucked the money into a pocket. "Sure. You sure you're okay?"

"It's been a helluva day, that's all." She tipped her head towards the tables. "Just make sure he's well taken care of."

"Will do."

She stepped into the bathroom and splashed cold water against her face, cooling it in an instant. She kept her head over the sink and let the droplets fall. Each drip matched with a breath. Another splash. More breaths. A few minutes passed, and she felt in control again. The tears had stopped, no longer running with the cool water. Her heart returned to a normal pace. Even her breathing was less laboured.

I'll be okay. I survived the ride. In one piece.

The paper towel scratched as it skidded over her tender skin. Tossing it, she studied herself in the mirror. Pale as a ghost, she gently pinched some colour back into her cheeks and gave them a quick rub.

The tips of her fingers palpitated under her bottom lashes, hoping to reduce the puffiness, and maybe take the darkening circles and bags away. Using her hand as a weak substitute for a comb, she ran it through her long dark hair, attempting to reduce the flyway's and stray strands that had escaped from the braid. It wasn't working and she pulled it apart, preferring a high ponytail instead.

Feeling more secure, she stepped outside the bathroom, spotting Lucas in a heartbeat. He was on the phone, so she hung back to let him finish the conversation.

How would she ever begin to repay him for everything he did for her? There was no doubt in her mind he was as emotionally wrung out as she was. He was worn down and beat up. God bless him though. Today was a dark day, and she was grateful he sat in the restaurant waiting for her. He hadn't run when she hit bottom. Not like her ex-boyfriend, Derek.

❤ Chapter Four ❤

"Aurora, please have a seat."

This therapist was older than the last. Way older than Chris and probably, if she were being honest, as old as her daddy. All the previous shrinks she'd seen had all been young and unsuccessful. Well, unsuccessful in helping her, as their wild ideas positively *sucked*.

The older man ambled over to his desk and grabbed her folder before he sat across from her on one of the two couches in the room. "I've been updated about your issues."

In order to avoid rolling her eyes in his face, she shut them instead.

"I understand what my colleagues have suggested and tried. But I'd like you to answer a few questions for me."

"Okay." Re-focusing on him, she kicked out of her shoes and pulled her legs under her. "I hate wearing shoes."

The couch caved beneath his mass as he readjusted himself. "Doesn't bother me. I'm glad you're getting comfortable."

"Oh, I'm hardly comfortable. I've been passed around from shrink to shrink week after week."

"Ah yes, something I'd like to address." A brief peek into her folder and then he tossed it on the table beside him. "I'm the fourth person you've seen in this office."

"Fifth, actually."

"Right. Forgive me. I wasn't including Dr. Johnson." He grabbed for a notepad. "Any reason why you keep changing doctors?"

A soft snort. "No one seems helpful. The techniques they've suggested aren't working."

"And how do you know that?"

"Because they're not," she said tersely.

His forehead puckered, broadcasting years of wrinkles. "Okay. You've worked on a few mental techniques like hypnosis, some role-playing and one attempt at shock therapy. Is that right?"

"Yeah."

"And you've yet to get into a vehicle."

She leaned on the armrest and sighed. "That's not entirely true anymore. I'm finally riding in a car."

He flipped through the folder, surveying each page. "Excellent. When did that happen?"

"Ten days ago."

His face brightened as his pen scratched across a pad of paper. "I'd say something worked. Tell me about it, since there's been no mention of it."

"Of course there wouldn't be. Dr. Donovan spent more time pushing back on her cuticles than she did listening. To test her, I even mentioned how Elvis walked into the room. After that, I'll be damned if I was going to share anything personal with her."

"Dr. Donovan was having a bad week."

"Well, she lost a patient. If she wasn't able to concentrate at work, she should've taken time off."

"She did." He hunched forward a bit. "But we're not here to talk about her. We're here to discuss you, and I'd like to know more about how you did riding in the car with Lucas."

Breaking eye contact with him, she shrugged. "It was short. I think, like, two minutes. Lucas drove us down the street."

"Tell me what you were thinking."

"I was scared obviously. Wasn't sure if I could do it."

"But you did. How?"

How? Well, I was angry for starters. Stupid weakness. And shame, lots and lots of shame.

Uncontrollable flushes of heat washed over her as she remembered, but she wasn't interested in delving into that topic right now. One thing at a time. In a quiet voice she said, "With Nate's help."

He reached for the file and peeked inside. "Ah, yes, the want-to-be boyfriend."

She growled under her breath. "Whatever."

"He was there?"

"In my mind. I could see him as if he was standing in front me, which obviously he couldn't do as we were driving."

"Interesting." The pen scribbled frantically in his hand. "And what was he doing?"

"Encouraging me. Smiling at me."

"Uh-huh. I see. And Lucas, what was he doing at that moment?"

"Driving of course." Uncomfortable sitting as she was, she twisted in her seat and stuck her legs out in front of her. Damn hip. As much as physio helped, the aching never went away. However, it was tolerable, and didn't *require* a Percocet for it. Not that she'd turn *that* down.

She glanced at the clock.

Not even close to being finished.

Air rushed out of her lungs. "I know where you're going with this."

I've been to enough therapy sessions to know what comes next.

"You think, and you're probably right, that I saw Nate's face, but it was Lucas' words. But it doesn't matter. The point is I got to the pub, and I got home. In one piece. Alive."

He studied her and turned down the pad of paper. "Are you grateful for that?"

"For getting home alive?" She narrowed her eyes. "Of course I am."

"Good. It seems to me my colleagues think discussing the actual accident will help, but that hasn't been the case, has it?"

Her body rippled with a violent shudder. She'd been over the accident so many times, from different points of view, and yet, it never got easier to talk about. The accident had been her fault even though the drunk driver of the other car ran the stop sign. Had she been paying attention, her passengers could've lived. She shuddered again.

"I'd like to take a different approach. I want you to tell me about your feelings. Not during the accident, but after. What was going through your mind?"

Oh great, he's one of those. A feelings shrink. Let's discuss emotions. Gag. Looks like I'll be seeing another shrink next week.

Her focus left him and searched out the room. Nothing out of the ordinary. A few full bookshelves. Framed diplomas hung on the wall. Vases full of what she presumed were fake flowers based on the level of dust. The furniture was more than a few years old and the table between them very weathered, its edges worn down. A lone tissue box decorated it.

"Does it bother you, me asking about after the accident?"

"There's not much to tell. I was in the hospital, drugged up, trying to heal. People came and visited, more out of obligation I think than anything else."

"Why do you think that?"

"Because no one wants to visit a monster. They come once just to see the extent of the damage with their own eyes. Then they leave and don't come back. After a couple of weeks, people just stopped coming around."

"Are you saying you felt lonely?"

She glared at him. "Wouldn't you?"

"Physically, you were recovering. Bones were setting and healing well?"

"I wouldn't say that. My pelvis never healed right and now I walk with a bit of a limp." She wanted to stand up and walk around just to prove it to him, but thought better of it and remained in her seat.

"Ah, yes. We'll get to that. So, you're in the hospital where your physical needs were being attended to. What about your mental needs? Did a psychologist ever come visit you?" His pencil tapped against his thigh.

"No, not that I'm aware of." She leaned back, and re-crossed her legs.

"At no point during your stay?"

"I don't think you understand how hospitals work. They treat you and street you. As fast as possible. There's no hand holding. No comforts. Just heal and get out."

"I hear the hostility in your voice."

"You should." She checked her phone.

Damn, we're not even close to being done.

"It wasn't the best time of my life. I missed my momma and sister's funerals. I missed my high school grad. The hospital I was recovering in was four hours away, so none of my hometown friends came to see me, at least not right away."

"Let's discuss that. Who did come to visit you?"

Her throat cleared, and she frowned in his direction. "My boyfriend at the time. My daddy. A few family members. Some girls from high school, but that was only once. After seeing the sour, piteous looks on their faces, I told Derek to tell them not to come back for a while. I wanted to be me again, or whoever I was milliseconds before the crash."

He reached for the note pad again, the eraser bopping against the paper. "And who was that?"

"Just a girl I once knew." Images floated through her head from another time, another place. "She was popular without being popular, know what I mean? Everyone knew her, but she wasn't part of any clique. She moved freely between groups, blending seamlessly into them as she wanted. She was a bright student, top of her class, heading into med school, *going* to make her mark on the world. Change it for the better. Not the best athlete but she somehow made it onto the volleyball team, which made it into the city finals. Apparently they won gold in provincials, but she wasn't there for that. Her boyfriend was Mr. Popular, the best singer in glee club and the leader of the robotics club. He gave up his graduation to stay by her side."

"That was nice of him."

"But it haunted him. I know it did. It was three weeks after my accident when he left. Three whole weeks. Twenty-one days." Sadness consumed her. It was amazing, two years later and that sting still hadn't left.

"If we may go back for a sec… When you talk about yourself before the accident, you speak in third person, and after the accident, you're back to first person."

A dull headache formed over her forehead and she pinched the bridge of her nose. "So?"

"It's interesting. You talk about her like she was someone else."

"She was." Her mouth twisted into a sour expression. "That's not me. That girl was everything and had the world before her. Anything she wanted was within grasp. This girl, the one sitting before you, has none of that. Everything now is a stretch. An impossible one."

"Let's focus on that for a minute. This other you, the before you, was a happy-go-lucky lady, am I correct?"

She nodded.

"And this current one, is depressed, going through some serious withdrawal issues, and I'm not talking about the drug issues which we will get to in a bit. Do you find it hard to make it through the day?"

Her eyes widened, and she stared at him.

"That's what I figured." He sat back in his chair but leaned forward. He tapped the pencil some more. "Let me ask you something. Are you happy to be alive?"

❤ Chapter Five ❤

W *here the hell did that come from? Of course I'm happy to be alive, you idiot. Sure, there was a long time after the accident where I waited for death and, in fact, welcomed it, but like everything else, death too avoided me. That was then, this is now.*

She stared at the shrink in shock. "Yes, I'm happy to be alive. Of course I am."

He leaned back, a small smirk on his wide face. "Good. Then that makes your homework easier."

"You're giving me homework?"

What kind of sick shrink dispenses homework? Where are all the drug dispensing shrinks? Why can't I see them?

"Yes. If you plan on coming back, I'd like to meet with you twice a week." Standing, he walked over to a bureau tucked in behind the chair, and opened a drawer. "I think we can make some great progress." With a piece of paper gripped in his hands, he walked back and sat across from her. "Your homework."

She read the top line.

Fifty things that make me happy.

"Is this a joke? What is this?"

"I want you to go home and fill it in."

"For real?"

"Absolutely. I think you have some deep-seated depression along with a few other concerns, but I see a lot of bright spots. Rather than focus on the negative, we're going to punctuate the positive. Draw on it." A chubby finger pointed to the paper. "But only you can tell me what needs to be on the list. And it can be anything. Something small or something huge." He nodded at her. "This list will be a lot of work."

She read it over again, unable to concentrate on the two columns of twenty-five lines.

Fifty is totally doable. Hell, I'll even shoot for a hundred just to prove something to this idiot.

"When do you want it finished by?" She folded it and tucked it into her purse.

"Our next appointment. Check with the receptionist if there's anything available on Monday or Tuesday. It'll give you time to work on it."

She stood. "I assume we're done?"

"For today."

She extended her hand. "Thank you, Dr. Navin."

He eyed her. "See you next week?"

"If I can finish the list." She forced a smile and left the office.

"Fifty things? Easy enough to do," Kaitlyn said at the entrance to the clinic.

Aurora wasn't sure if Kaitlyn came to all her appointments to make sure she actually went, or if it was to support her. Regardless, since Kaitlyn's trip to Russia, Aurora hadn't missed a single one. And as Lucas worked daily from nine until two, he couldn't escort her to therapy. Thank goodness. He would've insisted on driving. It was after all a prime training session. The only shrink availability was late morning and Kaitlyn claimed she could use the walk since she felt she'd packed on a few pounds on her holiday. Whatever the *real* reason was, she was grateful for the company on the long walk.

It was cooler in the office, so she'd kept a light sweater on, but now, under the heat of the daytime sun, she tied it around her waist. She didn't care if her scars were visible to the outside world, it was too damn hot for covered arms.

She wiped her forearm across her brow and fanned herself. "Could it be any hotter?"

"Well," Kaitlyn said with a shrug, "it could be forty below and we're walking home."

"Hopefully, when it's that cold, I'll be able to handle car rides, or bus rides at the very least."

That gives me what? A good four months? Shit.

Kaitlyn nudged her playfully. "Hopefully."

They walked through a path that took them underneath the shade of giant willows and oaks.

"How are things going in the car department?" she asked.

"About the same as before. It takes way longer to prepare for the trip than the actual trip."

"How so?"

"All the mental prep, the talking it out, where we're going, how we'll get there… That takes much longer than the actual driving."

"Yeah? But it's getting easier each time, right?"

Aurora shook her head and billowed her shirt.

"You've got what? Six weeks until the big day? There's still lots of time."

Her head dropped, and tendrils of dark hair fell against her sweaty cheeks. "Doesn't feel like it. This big date is circled on my calendar, taunting me. We were up until one in the morning driving around. Trying desperately to get some distance."

"How far did you get?"

"About five minutes away."

"What's going on?" Kaitlyn's full gaze fixed on her.

A small cloud of shame covered her. "I black out. Totally. Without warning. No black edges on the fringe. Just bam!" She clapped her hands together. "Out like a light."

"Shit. How scary, for both of you."

"I know." Her pace sped up a little. She itched to get to her apartment. It was ten blocks away still. At least it was air-conditioned because the heat was crushing her. "Sometimes I feel like it's never going to happen."

"It will. Somehow."

"But…"

Kaitlyn stepped in front of her. The sudden stop forced Aurora to balance on her tiptoes so she didn't crash into her friend. "Now you stop. You and Lucas have been working like maniacs on this. You've come so far." Kaitlyn's hands squeezed her shoulders. "You. Are. Riding. In. A. Car. You weren't doing that before, were you?"

She shrugged out of her grip and walked around her. "Why do you have to be like that?"

"Like what?"

She didn't need to glance at her to know there was a giant smirk on her face. She heard it loud and clear in her voice. "Always right."

"It comes with practice." Kaitlyn skipped to catch up.

She couldn't help it, Kaitlyn's comment made the laughter bubble out. The thing she loved about Kaitlyn the most was how she just knew how to react. Knew when a situation warranted breaking the tension with a witty comment, or when it warranted the cold, harsh, ugly truth. Digging through her purse, Aurora found a pen, and the dreaded list. A smile bloomed as she scratched Kaitlyn's name onto one of the blank spaces.

Kaitlyn peered over her shoulder. "What's that for?"

"You're one of the things that make me smile."

"Well, duh." She laughed and linked her arm with Aurora's. "So what's the game plan for the weekend?"

"So much. I have physio this afternoon, and then Lucas has something in store. Maybe tonight we'll try for a longer trip. I don't know."

"Are you staying clean?"

It had been hard admitting to Kaitlyn how she'd fallen and taken the 'easy way out' rather than ask for help. The resulting lecture she received had been an earful. However, she'd take it any day over the chewing out she got from Daddy. It took a lot of courage on her part to call him. She broke down and admitted everything.

To say he was livid would be a giant understatement. It took a lot of convincing to get him to stay put in Fort McMurray, and not skip out on work, drive down there and show her how wrong she was. In place of that version of hell, she now had to call daily. One screw up or missed call, and he'd be there to straighten her out, which was code for hospitalization. Indefinitely.

"Of course, but it's hard. Real hard. If I'm lucky, all I'll get is an Advil from physio. I miss my Percs. Lucas watches me like a hawk.

Chris still only dispenses me my two little Xanax each week, and she refuses to up it. I feel like I'm under lock and key."

Kaitlyn raised an eyebrow. "Don't you feel you brought that on yourself?"

"Maybe. But still. One wouldn't hurt." They crossed the street in silence, cars zooming by them on the left.

"Your drug habit was a little scary, Aurora."

Yeah, I know. No one lets me forget. Sheesh. One bad night where I ingested a combo of pills and you drove a crazy me home from the track. I get it, it was bad.

On the street corner, she pulled Kaitlyn to a stop. "I'm sorry."

"It's okay."

Her eyes searched Kaitlyn's. It was important her friend heard this. "No, it's not. For everything that happened before, I'm sorry. I was really messed up. I was an evil person who did really bad things."

"Aurora, you were never evil, and you aren't now. Yes, you were messed up. Like really messed up, but you didn't do anything bad."

The light turned green.

"Oh yes I did." Aurora marched across the busy road. "And you know it."

Kaitlyn didn't reply.

Aurora's feet touched the curb and she turned around where Kaitlyn still stood at the edge of the road. She waved her hands frantically and Kaitlyn raced over.

"But that's in the past. It's over and done, right? You have no further contact with the scumbag?" Kaitlyn hated Matthew. With a passion. If hate were people, she'd be China. Kaitlyn blamed Matthew for the relapse.

"Nothing further. Trial's over, so that's the end of that."

"What about the big library celebration?"

"Didn't I tell you?" A small laugh bubbled up from out of her. "I quit when he tried to kiss me."

Kaitlyn came to an abrupt halt. "Damn girl! Look at you go, you're changing your life one major thing at a time." She grabbed her friend's arm. "What are you going to do for a job now?"

"Well, Daddy pays the rent and sends me money for food, so it's mostly just my personal expenses I have to worry about. So it's not like I *need* a job. And with the lack of available nearby options…"

They passed a few stores on their right. A run down strip mall that housed a restaurant with décor straight from the 1960s, a chain hair salon, a liquor store, a dry cleaners and a tanning salon, which a bronzed brunette exited.

"I've no desire to work at any of these places." She thumbed towards the stores. "So, I've been taking on more jobs with PDR gaming."

"What's PDR Gaming?"

"Geez, I thought I told you this?"

The sun glinted off the steel balcony of her apartment as they approached. A breeze ghosted by and she faced into it, revelling in the momentary cool.

"Well, you promise not to laugh?" She watched and waited for a smile that never came.

A wrinkle of confusion surfaced on Kaitlyn's face.

"Okay, before you think I've completely lost my mind, PDR Gaming is a product, development and research gaming corporation. I'm a beta tester for their apps."

"You and your gaming." Kaitlyn rolled her eyes. "That's an odd job."

"Not really. With Lucas gone every weekend and during the day for a few hours, it gives me time to play, or work as they call it. I pick and choose different gigs from the job-board. The pay isn't great, but it's consistent. I'm setting aside half my earnings for the Lucas Johnson Car Trust."

"You what? Wow."

Pride bubbled in her. "He spends all his free time with me, so this is just a little something. It's not going to be big money, but I hope it'll help."

Kaitlyn licked her lips, and a spring formed in her walk. It was as if she were dancing. "You're sweet to do that. I'm sure he'll appreciate it."

"I'm hopeful. Racing is so expensive. Just the other week, he mentioned Nate needed some engine work and how much it was going to drain the bank account."

"Yeah, that shit's pricey." Kaitlyn raised an eyebrow and pulled her to a halt. "How's that going to work getting you to the U of A if you're not able to ride in cars yet?"

"Yeah, I've been thinking about that. Most of the classes I can take online and then I'll be able to transfer over when I get to the point of handling that long of a car ride. It won't be as easy, but at least I can wear jammies to school." She laughed.

It wasn't ideal, and she knew firsthand she didn't have the dedication to focus on online work. That failed miserably with the classes she had tried to take last semester. Holding back on her courses wasn't an option, especially with her daddy still covering the expenses, so it limited her.

"Lucas hopes I'll be ready for that drive on day one, but I think he's really reaching. We just can't make it past the five-minute point right now, let alone a traffic-free fifteen-minute ride."

She had little faith she'd be able to make the trip to the U of A before the end of term which really worried her. If she couldn't handle that, how the hell was she going to make the forty-five-minute trek to the track? No matter what they tried, at five minutes her body and mind forced an abrupt end to that particular training session. The blackouts were ridiculous.

"Well, I'm glad you're not giving up."

"Speaking of not giving up..." She raised a brow and turned.

"Nope. Not going there." Kaitlyn's pace changed into a march, and she made good time putting distance between them.

She hobbled to grab a hold of her friend. "Oh sure, me we can dissect until I'm bleeding and raw, but I ask anything of you–"

"It's not up for discussion, Aurora."

"The hell it's not." She snagged the back of Kaitlyn's shirt, spinning her around. "They're your parents. You need to tell them. Especially now."

"I don't *need* to tell them anything." Kaitlyn's voice filled with raw emotion. "They've stated in as many words that homosexuality is a sin, and I've watched them turn their backs on friends who've come out. I don't want to lose them." Her eyes went glassy.

"But you're their daughter. They'll still love you."

"No they won't. To them I'll be a sinner, someone they can never be with. According to them and the bible, I'll never get into heaven because I'm evil. I'm destined for hell. They'd accept your drug addiction before they'd ever accept the fact that I'm a lesbian."

"Kaitlyn," she said in the softest tone.

"It's true." Kaitlyn stormed ahead of her.

By the way her shoulders rolled inward, Aurora knew her friend was crying. And she couldn't hobble fast enough to catch up.

Eventually, Kaitlyn slowed down and Aurora was able to get close enough to link arms. "What about Tatiana? She's coming to visit you, right?"

"So?"

"So? Don't you think you ought to tell your parents about the true reason for the visit? If I can tell Daddy about my relapse, you should be able to tell them about the woman you've fallen in love with."

Tears smeared across her high cheekbones. "I do love her, but I don't know if I can break up my family for her."

Aurora sighed. Yes, that would be a tough decision. She hardly knew Kaitlyn's family, but couldn't wrap her head around how any parent would disown a child based on sexual orientation. "I'll make you a deal. If I can make it to the track without passing out, you tell your parents."

Kaitlyn tied her blond hair into a quick knot at the base of her neck. "It's not that easy."

She laughed. "You're telling me? I can't make it beyond five minutes. Forty-five will be the death of me."

Kaitlyn narrowed her eyes. "No deal. If you die, I lose. If you survive the trip, I still lose."

"What are you going to do? Marry her first, then tell your parents?"

She clapped her hands together. "I got it. I'll wait until we've adopted boatloads of children first."

"You're hopeless, you know that?" Aurora wiped the building sweat off her forehead. "I love you, but you're completely hopeless."

"Yeah." Kaitlyn nudged her. "Hopelessly in love. Just like you." She nodded to the main entrance of the apartment. "Let's get upstairs and cool down."

❤ Chapter Six ❤

Lucas squatted in front of her DVD player and fiddled with opening a case.

"We're not going to watch a home movie, are we?" Aurora asked.

The case was black, and devoid of text. Definitely home made, but despite her quip, she doubted it was something from their childhood.

He laughed at her question. "No, not a home movie."

"Good, because I'm not in the mood for that."

"You could be. I'm sure Mom has some very interesting movies with Nate as a little boy. He was a reckless one, quite the daredevil."

Sigh, Nate. Oh how she missed him. This torture she inflicted on herself day after day had better be worth it. She'd better get her man at the end.

Lucas stood up, concern etching across his features. "Don't go there."

"I wasn't going anywhere."

"I can see it all over your face."

The couch squeaked as she sank further into it. "Is he still..." She didn't *really* want to know, but sort of did. "Is he still with her?"

He turned his focus back to the DVD player and turned on the TV. "Yes." His voice a low grumble.

"Oh." She swallowed hard, and an ache started to build deep in her chest.

"Yeah, I agree. He's never home anymore."

She raised an eyebrow and folded her arms across her body. "How would you know? You're never there yourself."

"Touché." He grabbed the remote off the table. "Mom's mentioned it."

Her heart stopped. She figured Nate would hang out with his girlfriend, she just didn't think it would be that often. That meant Nate was with Marissa more than Aurora realized. Jealousy filled her soul. She wasn't even happy if he was happy, if he was in fact happy. She wanted him, and she didn't want him with anyone else. All summer, she'd been wrestling her fears to show him that she could handle the racing life, and not die each time something went wrong. It was tough, but in her mind, he was totally worth it.

Aurora connected with Lucas.

"Wait... if he's with Marissa..." Her thoughts swirled at 100 mph. "Does this mean..." It *can't*. "Does this mean he's given up..." Her mouth dried up and her saliva turned to cotton. "The idea of retirement?"

Lucas fidgeted and averted his gaze.

"Oh." She thrust a hand through her hair and gave it a tousle. "So, what's the point of doing this? Of trying to impress him if he wants nothing to do with me and he's going to stay doing what he loves?"

"Because it's not gonna last. He needs you."

"How can you be so sure?"

"I'm not supposed to tell you this, but since I've opened my big fat mouth, you might as well know." He avoided peering in her direction as his index finger tapped against his bottom lip. After a few breaths he rubbed his hand over his shirt. Right over his heart. "He's started his own racing company, and he named it after you."

Her eyes widened, and she leaned forward. "What? Me?"

"Northern Lights Racing." He sat down on her weathered sofa. "No offense, but it has a nicer ring to it than Aurora Racing."

Aha. The day she met Nate and he'd learned of her name, he wondered if she was named after the celestial occurrence. "I'm... speechless."

"Finally," he cheered and raised his hands into the air as he winked. "Just kidding."

"He's going to run his own company and race? I'm missing something."

"It's complicated but I'll see if I can make it make sense. He branded the name and bought the domain just after you broke up. He's been talking with various companies in hopes of sponsorship for Northern Lights Racing, but before they take him on, he needs to prove himself. Which he's been doing well. Until Marissa."

That bitch. Screwing him up. Screwing him. Ugh.

"She's messing with him and he's not doing as well in points."

"And that's why you don't think they're going to last? He's going to break up with her because he's not winning?"

That doesn't sound like the Nate I know.

"It's more than that. They argue quite a bit on race nights, and I think that's throwing him off. He needs tranquility before a race to allow him to get into the zone, and she's not providing it." His gaze fell. "With you, he was upbeat and happy. With her, he's angry and miserable. He needs you, and he wants you. He's still out there trying to get Northern Lights Racing up off the ground so he can still be involved with racing if he's not in the driver's seat."

So he can still be a part of what he loves without me freaking out.

Thinking of Nate with his lit up face, dimpled smile, and sexy as hell race suit, made her heart ache. She needed to get him off her mind. And quickly. Loneliness was like a bad disease, spreading slowly through her veins. In an attempt to delay the pinpricks of pain around her heart, she focused on Lucas. "So what wonderful low-budget production are we watching? Do I need to make popcorn?"

Popcorn sounds really amazing right now.

The smell of melted butter tickled the senses of her brain.

Lucas flopped down beside her. "I think you'll want to avoid eating for a bit."

Her swallow was audible. "It's not a horror, is it? I hate horror movies."

A small smirk appeared at the corner of his lips. "Not a horror." His eyes twinkled in the sunlit room, highlighting the tinges of blue. "It's something Chris and I discussed, and we'll see how it goes."

Lucas and Chris discussed her training sessions?

"Why am I suddenly scared?"

"You remember that one shrink who suggested writing down all your fears associated with vehicles?"

She rolled her eyes. "How could I forget?"

What was it with shrinks and lists? They had made a list of forty-three different fears ranging from something as simple as a fear of throwing up in front of someone, to death. It had been quite eye opening. To everyone. Lucas included.

"Well, we're gonna go through some of them."

A halt to her voice. "Like what?" She choked out the words as her mouth suddenly dried up. What fear were they going to cover now? Truly, they really had been working hard on them. She was trying hard to avoid the death one though.

"We're gonna watch some videos on safety mechanics and then watch a few car crashes."

"We're going to do *what*?" Her voice pitched to a near shrill.

Lucas slapped his knees as he sunk in his spot beside her. "It'll show you how safe and protected we are."

Her heart fell into the depths of her stomach. "Nuh-uh."

"Look, if it gets too scary, we'll just turn it off."

Slowly, her gaze travelled from Lucas' adoring face to the small screen in front of them. She forced herself to blink, swallow and breathe. Pulling the blanket tight around her as the air temperature dropped, she nodded. *I can do this.*

"Turn it off, please," she said, burying her head under Lucas' arm.

With a quick flick of the remote, the TV went black.

"I don't feel good," she said.

Lucas stood up and disappeared, returning a moment later with a glass of water and a washcloth. He lifted her hair and draped the cool cloth around her nape.

A chill washed over her. "That feels nice."

"Drink." He sat beside her and passed her the glass.

She sipped the water back and leaned against the sofa. "That video was too much. Way too much."

It was akin to a 'Best Of' reel. Best NASCAR crashes of the past five years. It was horrifically spectacular.

"What are you feeling?"

Unable to look at him, she focused on her thoughts. "Fear mostly, but it's different. Definitely not the same fear as I have getting into a car, but still."

It was hard to describe. It turned her cold, made her nauseous, yet, it didn't make her heart race uncontrollably.

"It has to be fear. Yeah, it's fear." Although she wasn't a hundred percent sure on that.

"Okay, that's normal. I think. But you saw how everyone survived?"

"Yes. Especially that Austin guy. That was really hard to watch. Over and over."

A race car travelling at nearly 200 mph was touched by another car, resulting in his car flipping over two other rows of cars, and into a catch fence, stopping dead on the track. Until another car ran into the smashed up car, sending it spinning across the grass. It was horrific to watch. But the most amazing thing, the thing Lucas really wanted to drive home, was how the driver walked away from the accident.

"That was a spectacular crash he survived," Aurora said.

And he did. Bruised up, she was sure, but nothing broken. Not even his spirit as he was back on the track in no time. Yet, two years after her crash...

Through one open eye, she glared at him before shutting his smirk away. A deep sigh and she readjusted herself, billowing her shirt as her feet hit the floor.

"Why aren't regular cars equipped the same way?"

"It's expensive. Plus, as a rule, no one drives at 200 miles per hour."

A yawn escaped her; fear was exhausting. "Do you think if Momma and Carmen were in a car with all those safety systems—do you think they would've lived?"

Lucas ran a hand through his strawberry-blond hair, leaving a few wayward strands standing straight up. "I don't know. Maybe? You're comparing apples to oranges. You survived, right?"

Yes, she had. Barely. But it never stopped the what-ifs. It was a game she played all the time. What if they had those safety systems? What if they'd left even a few seconds later? Or what if they had taken a different route? What if Carmen had drove instead of her? An image of her big sister, floated through her mind. She sang along in the backseat of the car, her off-tune voice floating through the interior. So carefree, so young.

Aurora's breath did a double skip as the images crashed over her. "I miss them." The heel of her hand rubbed over her heart. "So much."

"I know you do."

The tears started to fall. Another vision, one of Momma as she smiled at her, singing along to the old Martina McBride song on the radio.

"Come here," Lucas said, lifting up his arm.

She cradled into his chest and allowed the tears to keep falling. One of her shrinks had said it was healing to let the tears fall. She wasn't feeling healed by any stretch, but it felt good all the same.

Oh, what she wouldn't give for a time machine. To go back to that night and leave just a few seconds earlier. Or later. Any amount of time differential would mean that they would be here now, instead of up in heaven. And she'd be living a normal life.

His hand ran over her head, smoothing down her hair. "It'll be okay. We'll get you through this."

"I know." She sniffed. Not wanting to leave the sanctity of his warmth, she curled in a little more, his chest rising up and down with his breaths. "I have homework from my shrink, this new one, and I'm struggling to get it done."

His hand moved to her shoulder, giving it a little squeeze.

"He asked if I was happy to be alive," she said.

"That's a weird question to ask, isn't it?"

"I thought so too, and yet I haven't been able to get it out of my mind. It's one of the many things keeping me awake at night."

"Yeah, there's no end to the things you torture yourself over."

She dismissed his comment. It wasn't her fault the dreams were so vivid. If she had any choice, she'd prefer to sleep but her mind just won't shut up. The Benedryl helped, but it was no longer an option. "I keep going back to that question. It's like it hangs over me, constantly questioning me. I think I am happy to be alive, but I'm not really."

"What?" He shifted slightly beside her.

"Well, you see, after the accident, I was a mess. A total wreck. I was in the hospital, bandaged up, pins sticking out of me. At one point I had a respirator to help me breathe. I was a living Frankenstein."

Before the curtain pulled back, she'd heard whisperings from the staff to keep things upbeat and show no expressions. Human instinct is not something you can control. The first time Daddy saw her, he made the most horrific expression. It didn't matter if it lasted microseconds, she saw it. Guilt, shame, horror–it all flashed across his face before the fatherly compassion surfaced once again.

"I remember laying there, in the middle of the night, no one around. The heart monitor beside me beeping out each beat. The rest of the room was void of sound. No echoes of shoes on the floor, no chatter of nurses in the background. Just this eerie fucking silence. And I got an itch on my leg. Due to my pincushion surrounding my hips, I couldn't scratch it as I couldn't bend at the waist. I was helpless. Totally helpless. And very much alone." She picked at the lettering on Lucas' shirt. "No one knew I was itchy. Then the itch started to hurt. But I was still alone."

"That must've been terrible."

"It gets worse." His large inhale of air pushed her up. With the release of air, she closed her eyes. The image of that dark night froze on her brain like a movie on pause. "It had been almost a month. I was still in the hospital. Anything I needed done, I needed to have a nurse do it. I couldn't even wipe my own ass. Do you know how humiliating that is? I couldn't take care of my own basic needs. I had staff to help feed me for a bit once I was off the respirator."

"That's... wow. I'm really sorry." His voice soft, yet almost disbelieving.

"So that night, I was laying there. Helpless. And I felt sorry for myself. Wondered if I was ever going to heal. Everything felt so grim and I know now that I was at rock bottom." She wrapped a fallen strand of hair around her ear. In a low voice, she carried on. "My boyfriend had just left me. My so-called friends hadn't been by in weeks. Daddy came when he could, but he still had things to do. He had planned not one, but two funerals. He was trying to settle Carmen's affairs, and Momma's to a point. Somewhere in there, he tried to visit his injured daughter in a hospital four hours away, but I really wasn't the best company."

Lucas' grip intensified on her shoulder, pulling her in tighter.

"That night..." She sighed, her heart aching at the memory of it. "I wished for death. I begged for it. I surrendered to it. Told Death to come and take me away. I felt like I was living in hell and I didn't want to live like that. I'd rather be dead."

His swallow was audible. "How long did you..."

"Months. The shrinks I saw said my depression was normal, came with the accident. Here, try this pill, it'll help, they said. Take this one too, it'll make you forget." A sassiness to her voice as she remembered the white coats and their arsenal of drugs. "It's all normal, they claimed. You'll get over it soon. But you know what's not normal? Wanting death. Trying to find a way to get it when it ignores you. But I had no control. The only thing I could control was what I ate. And when I tried starving myself, the nurses hooked me up to fluids. There went that. I had no control over anything." She pushed herself up and wiped her face. "Finally, I caved. And they were right. The drugs helped. Ah, those were good. They numbed me. Numbed my feelings. Numbed the joke of a life I now lived."

Lucas gasped at her revelations. He reached out for her hand and held it tightly. "If it's any consolation, I'm glad you chose life."

"That's the thing. I didn't choose life. Death just never came for me." She couldn't stand facing in his direction any more and watch the hurt blossoming behind his grey-blues with such force. A heartbeat was all it took for her to understand that his expression wasn't one of hurt, it was of pity. "Please don't look at me like that."

"I'm... I'm sorry." He didn't let go of her hand and gave it a tender rub. "I don't know what to say."

She shrugged, her heart empty. "There's nothing to say. I know you're trying to be all sweet and see the good in everything, because that's who you are. You're a great guy. And I'm... well, I'm just me."

His voice fell. "Aurora."

"It's true. And it's not me having another pity party, it's the iron-clad truth. I'm miserable. My life sucks. My mind is a scary place to be. My body aches. I depend on the wrong things."

"Where's all this coming from?"

"My shrink gave me homework. Told me to write down fifty things that make me happy. I've come up with six. SIX. All weekend long I've thought about it, and that's the best I could do. Six. Pathetic, isn't it?"

She stood up and walked over to the kitchen table. After a quick rifle through the stack of papers, she found the one she was searching for. She thrust it into Lucas' hand.

"Number one. Nate. Well, duh." An awkward smile teased at his lips. "Aw, thanks. I'm number two."

"Of course you are. You make me smile when I really don't want to."

"Three, Kaitlyn. Naturally." He winked. "Four, baking. Why yes, you're very good at that. Five, music. Anything in particular?" The paper flipped down.

"Do you think I should be more specific?"

"No, I personally was curious."

"I love Ed Sheeran, Taylor Swift–"

Lucas covered his mouth and faked a gag.

"Say or think what you want, her songs are catchy. And sometimes you just need to dance off nervous energy. It helps."

With his eyebrow cocked, he carried on. "And finally, oh…" His cheeks filled with colour, and he jumped off the couch as if he'd sat on a pin. The paper crumpled in his hands and he tossed it to the floor.

His reaction made her smile. Lucas always had the best reactions.

"Yeah, I put it on there. Sex makes me happy. Although I'm not getting any lately."

"Whoa, too much info for me," he said.

"But you're my best friend. I'm supposed to share this kind of thing with you."

"Not me," he said, tugging on his shirt collar. "Kaitlyn for sure."

"Yeah, well, the point is, I'm supposed to have fifty things on there by tomorrow. What a complete failure I am."

He grabbed the ball of paper, unfolding it as he walked to the table. With a pen in hand, he flipped the paper over and smoothed it out, scratching out the numbers one through ten. "Before your accident, would you say you were much happier?"

"Yeah."

"Okay. Let's start there. Tell me ten things that used to make you happy."

Too easy. "Carmen. Her clothes. She always had the best taste in clothing. I loved sneaking something out of her closet." As she remembered, her body relaxed. "Momma. The smell of her baking when I'd come home from school. The flowers she planted in the front garden, their smell always blasted you in the face when you'd walk outside."

"What flowers are those?"

"Hyacinth and something orange."

He scribbled those down. "Keep going."

She pulled out a chair and sat across from him. "Getting good grades in school. I used to be an honours student."

But not anymore.

For a quick breath, humiliation filled her entire being. She shook it off and focused back on the task. "Volleyball. That used to make me happy."

The sounds of a gymnasium full of cheering sounds replayed in her mind. God, her team had a lot of fun.

"This one sweater I used to have. It was the most beautiful shade of blue and the softest material. Just putting it on fresh from the dryer was awesome."

"Okay, a blue sweater." The pen scratched across the paper.

"A sunrise. A sunset. The waves crashing onto the shore."

He glanced up from the table for a brief moment. "Did you grow up by the ocean?"

"No. But I visited Hawaii once when I was thirteen, our first overseas trip. I loved it." The memory of it—the salt in the air, the pounding of the waves as they beat on the sand, the cold rush of water that threatened to wash her away—it all came forth as if she was there yesterday. A broad smile spread from ear to ear.

"I'm adding that one to your current list. Clearly it makes you happy still."

"Fine," she said, watching the pen fly across the paper. "Add that to the list."

"Anything else? Just off the top of your head."

"Gatherings with friends. I used to hang out with my friends all the time."

The pen dropped to the table and he crinkled up his brows. "You hang out with me. And Kaitlyn on occasion."

"True, but it's not the same. You and I, we're focused on a goal, trying to get something accomplished. With my friends, in the before times–"

Lucas snorted.

"We'd hang out just to hang out. No goals. No purpose. Just fun."

"And you and Kaitlyn never do that?" That infectious smirk caused her to giggle.

Yes, they had girl's nights. Usually once a month. "You got me. Add that to the current list."

"See, you just needed some help. I think you were over thinking it."

"Maybe." She walked over to him. Bending down, she gave him a hug and a light kiss on the cheek. "Thank you. For being you."

The heat on his cheeks warmed her lips. "You're welcome."

"Now, let me make you supper and then we're going to take another drive tonight. Let's break that five-minute mark."

❤ Chapter Seven ❤

The room she sat in didn't appear any different from when she was there last week, but yet, something about it was different. Perhaps it was smaller? But that'd be impossible right? The couches were in the exact same places, angled in such a way no matter where she sat, she'd be facing him. The antique-looking clock hung on the wall, ticking loudly in the otherwise silent room. A quick sniff revealed an aroma of stale coffee, and a hint of a peanut butter infused lunch. Completely the same, and yet, different. She couldn't figure out what it was.

Dr. Navin ambled into the room, after a quick knock. "Good afternoon, Aurora. Glad you made it in. I wasn't sure if you'd be coming back or not."

"You do have a patient call sheet to refer to, do you not?"

He halted. The door clicked, and he tossed her file on the desk behind the couch. "Of course we do, but that doesn't mean anything. Patients cancel at the last minute all the time."

"That can't be good for business."

"You're right, it's not. However, it does allow me more time to focus on the ones that do want to meet me, and do want the help, such as yourself. So there's that." He parked himself down on the couch across from her. "How was your weekend?"

"Well, I worked on your damn list."

"And?" His head cocked to the side as he leaned back. A pudgy hand fell softly onto his knee when he crossed his legs.

"It was difficult."

"It was meant to be."

"You made it sound like it would be easy. Something I could quickly write down."

"I never said that, and I never intended it either."

She huffed and rooted through her purse, extracting a crinkled sheet. Trying to smooth out the wrinkles, she passed it to him.

He flipped it over and held it up to the window.

Was he trying to be an ass and see through the small grease spot?

"It seems as if this piece of paper has seen better days."

"Yeah, many times I turned it into a ball and threw it against the wall."

"Let's go over it, shall we?"

Dr. Navin was impossible to read. His expression never lit up, and no smile threatened to erupt. His lips didn't even mumble as if in deep thought. Nothing. Not even a shift in position. He was a blank book.

"This is very interesting," he said.

"I'll bet." She fought the urge to roll her eyes.

"I'm curious to understand why you have Percocet and Xanax listed."

"You're the doctor. You should understand."

His body stiffened at the remark. "But I want you to explain it to me. Why do you have those two drugs listed?"

"You've seen my file, right? You know I am addicted to them." She pressed her hands against her thighs to stop fidgeting.

"Am? Or were?"

Hmm. She crossed her arms over her chest. "Both I suppose."

"Are you currently using?" He reached behind him to the desk and pulled over the manila file folder. His thumb brushed along the edge of multiple pages.

She cringed. Having already gone over the Benedryl incident with Lucas, Kaitlyn and her daddy, she really felt no need to go over it again, especially with someone who couldn't even understand her previous addiction to Percocet. Evasiveness was always the answer. "The Xanax? Yes. Chris, I mean Dr. Johnson, doses me two a week. But no to the Percs. However, it doesn't mean I'm not still addicted to them.

I think about them all the time. When I finally fall asleep, I dream of them."

"What is it about them you enjoy so much?"

So many reasons really.

She huffed and selected the best answer. The one that would probably end the questioning. "The way they take away my pain."

"Tell me about your pain."

He's relentless. Tell me about this. Talk about that. You're the doctor. You're supposed to know what all this means. Just tell me I'm crazy and call it a day.

Instead of lashing out, she changed positions. Twice. Aurora sat on her legs and hugged herself. "It's not just physical, because I get Advil after physio. It's mental too. And maybe a bit emotional. Just having the perc makes me not feel anything at all."

"What are you trying to avoid?"

"Feeling lost."

Dammit. That fell out too easily.

"Ah. Yes." The folder skidded onto the table between them. "And how do we avoid that feeling?"

"By taking the Percs?"

Seriously? How did this man ever graduate from medical school?

"Without drugs."

Oh.

She shifted in her seat, trying to find a comfortable position but it seemed pointless. Everything made her uncomfortable. "I don't know. Guess that's why I'm here to see you."

"Okay. So your top three things on your list include your former boyfriend–"

"Who I'm trying to win back."

"His brother."

"My new best friend."

"And your other best friend."

"Yes."

"How do you think we can use those three things to avoid feeling lost?"

She swallowed hard. Her eyes darted around the room, staying on an object only long enough to say its name. Cool air from the AC brushed over her shoulders, causing goosebumps to ripple across her arms. "I already spend a wicked tonne amount of time with Lucas. He practically lives in my apartment."

"Does that make you happy?"

Using her fingernail, she picked at the dry skin around her nails. "It doesn't bother me, if that's what you're getting at."

"When he's not there, do you feel alone?"

She got a good size piece of skin and gave it a solid rip. "Physically?"

"No. Mentally."

Ouch.

She put the bleeding finger in her mouth and sucked it clean, giving it a wipe on the edge of her sleeve. "It's nice having him there. It's comforting in many ways. But yeah, when he's gone, I feel it. And I hate that feeling."

"Of dependence?"

"Yes." The bleeding wouldn't stop. She reached for a tissue and pressed a wad of it against her finger.

"Why?"

"Because I'm just waiting for the day when he'll walk out the door and never come back. I know it's going to happen."

"Why?"

Her hands flailed through the air. "Because they all do. At some point, everyone walks out of my life. Derek did. My friends did. Nate did. It's only a matter of time before Lucas does too."

"Actually..." Dr. Navin reached for the folder once again. "If I read the notes correctly, you pushed Nate out. He never actually walked away."

"Well, he's not making any grand efforts to get back in now, is he? His planned retirement has since gone up in smoke. Just like his desire to be with me. I'm vapour." She pressed her back into the couch and crossed her arms over her chest, huffing slightly.

"What is it you'd like?"

Leaning forward, she said, "For once in my fucking life I'd like to be fought over. To feel special enough that someone wants to be with me, and they'll move heaven and earth to do it. To be heard when I speak up, and to know they hear me when I don't. I want to feel like I deserve a better life than the one I've been given."

"Maybe he is fighting for you, and you just don't know it."

"Really? He's dating another girl. He's not going to retire anymore. I'd say he's given up."

"Men are funny creatures."

"You're telling me."

"Maybe he wants you to be jealous?"

Eyes narrowed into tiny little slits, she said, "Yeah, and how does that work? Remember, as far as he knows I know nothing. He doesn't know Lucas and I are hanging out."

"Have you ever seen them together?"

"Who? Nate and Marissa?" She shook her head and readjusted. "No."

The shrink leaned forward, accusation clouding his voice. "Ever think that maybe Lucas is feeding you a line?"

A smidgen of doubt crept into her mind. There had been no evidence, just hearsay.

Jerk. How dare you?

She rubbed her neck to loosen the knot forming. "And what? Are you saying he's *acting* all pissed off whenever her name gets mentioned?"

"Perhaps he's doing it to make you jealous."

"Yeah, right. Why would he do that??"

"Because jealousy can make you do some crazy things, and also, some amazing things. Right now, you're trying to beat your PTSD. In a way, your jealousy fuels that push—that desire—to win against it."

Her jaw clenched as did her fists. "I'm not jealous of Nate's relationship. He can go on and make babies with Marissa for all I care." But she didn't believe that.

"Really? If that were the case, he wouldn't be the first thing on your list."

As her anger simmered, so did her tone. "He'd never have the life with me that he could have with her. Nate and I are so different, on so many levels. Marissa is everything I wish I could be."

"That's the jealousy talking."

"It is not." She shook her head "It's the truth. She's beautiful and into cars. She races them too. She's smart and can probably give Nate a dozen kids."

"So you're not into cars. Big deal. Opposites attract."

"Yes. The girl with vehicular post-traumatic stress disorder falls in love with a race car driver. You can't get much more opposite than that." A large sigh escaped her as she rolled her eyes.

"This is true." He leaned forward and put his elbows on his knees, steepling his fingers together. Seconds ticked by on the clock, their sound echoing throughout the room. Leaning back, he finally said, "Twice in the span of a minute you brought up someone giving Nate babies. Care to explain?"

She shrugged, brushing off his comment. "I'm incapable. The accident wrecked my uterus, and they removed it during one of the surgeries."

A simple nod, but one that had him reaching for the file folder once again. Pen in hand, he made a note on one of the papers. "Sorry. That should be in here. There's never been any mention of it."

"Because I don't make it a habit of telling people I can't have children."

The file folder hit the table once again. "Does Nate know?"

"Yes."

"Okay." He shifted in his seat. "Let's get back to the list, shall we?"

"Is it wrong?"

His attention deviated from the table up to her. "Is what wrong?" A tip from his head as the question hung in the air.

"Is it wrong to have Nate as my number one? Even though I'm not with him, and there's no future family with him if we ever got back together, is it wrong that he's still on my list? I mean, that would mean I'm putting my dependence on happiness into a guy rather than finding it on my own, right?"

"I think you read too much into this exercise."

She slumped back into the couch. "Yeah, that's what Lucas said too."

"It was meant to show you, or help remind you, of what makes you happy. Somewhere along the way, you lost those things. Depression took over, which is natural with what you went through. It's my job to help you get through that. To find a new lease on life. We're only on this planet for a short time in the grand scheme of things, why not make it the best we can? If…" His focus went to the crumpled piece of paper. "Listening to the waves crash on a beach makes you happy, then listen to them. There's lots of music with waves on it if you can't make it to a real beach." He slid forward. "Do the things that make you happy. Find out what makes your heart happy and focus on that. It's too easy to go down the rabbit hole of dark thoughts."

"You're telling me." Her foot tapped against the coffee table leg. That rabbit hole pulled her down deep not too long ago.

"I believe you can do it. I believe there's a fight in you. To win out against the drug use. Against the PTSD. To be the person you want to be."

She slumped back in her seat, arms folded tightly over her body. "How?"

"I have a plan."

❤ Chapter Eight ❤

Stretching and slowly working the kinks out, she ambled her way down the hall. Aurora peeked into the living room. Lucas' arm dangled off the couch as he slept. Soft snores escaped his partially opened mouth. She couldn't help but smile at the comical nature of it. With Nate it was different. She found it adorable. With Lucas, she wanted to grab a sharpie and draw a mustache on his face and snap a picture.

She got the coffee going, lingering over the tin as she inhaled the scent of dark roasted beans. Nothing much beat the smell of fresh coffee. Eager to start her day, she went back to the bedroom. As she walked by her dresser, she stopped and stared at the list of fifty things. Items were written down in a messy, cursive she wasn't familiar with.

Holding it up, she stared at the four new items.

#19 – having just enough milk for a bowl of cereal

#20 – the barista spelling your name right

#21 – the perfect turkey/cheese/mayo/cucumber sandwich

#22 – freshly brushed teeth

She laughed and read the words again. Someone was taking notes, and that someone was sleeping in her living room. What a guy.

After a hot shower and freshly scrubbed teeth, she poured herself a coffee and started breakfast. The aroma of batter and heated maple syrup permeated the air. Flipping a fresh pancake, she jumped when, from the corner of her eye, she saw movement.

"Geezus, Lucas. You frightened me."

He laughed, and stretched so high, his shirt rose above his belly button. "Sorry."

"No, it's okay." She flipped another pancake onto the serving plate. "Hope you're hungry."

"Indeed." He reached beside her and grabbed a couple of plates. "I saw the list."

He ran fingers through his untamed hair and smiled sheepishly at her. "What list?"

"Oh stop. You know."

"Yeah, I do." He winked.

"Are you taking notes on me?"

"No. I just happened to notice what made you smile. You made a comment yesterday at breakfast about the milk. Then there was that barista at GrabbaJoes who spelled your name correctly, and you got all giddy about it." He finished setting the table. "Your shrink said they don't have to be major things. Just whatever makes you happy. Sometimes the little things really are big things, and you just don't see them."

"A little early for being philosophical, isn't it?"

"Nah, it's after nine."

Aurora brought the stack of warm pancakes to the table and hesitated for a moment. "When was the last time you checked in with your mom?"

He seemed unfazed by it. "Am I staying here too much and this is your polite way of asking me to leave?"

"Lucas, you should know me better than that. I don't hide behind politeness."

He laughed and poured himself a cup of coffee.

"But really, doesn't she miss you or wonder where you are?"

"Do you think I should tell her the truth about what I'm doing?"

"Do you think that would bother her or do you think it would help smooth things out?"

"Meh." He sat down. "She knows I haven't run away and joined a circus."

"Ah, but you have." She laughed at her own comment. It certainly felt like she was part of a circus. A never-ending one at that.

His constant re-deflection of her questions and lack of answers irritated her. She knew better than to push. Surely Brenda and Lucas would see eye to eye. Eventually.

"I need to ask. Does it feel weird to be here when you could be at the track instead?"

Those grey-blues connected with hers. "Not really." He shrugged. "Maybe a little. But I'm not racing this weekend, and it's really hard to be around–"

Nate. Brenda. Marissa.

He didn't need to finish the sentence, she knew. Those three possibilities held him back. A smidgen of doubt nagged at her. Was he telling the truth? Or feeding her a line? Could he not go and at least watch? Why did Dr. Navin plant that seed, and worse, why was she buying it? She cleared her throat and pushed the pancakes around her plate.

"Anyway, he doesn't need me there tonight. With her hanging out in our space all the time, I'm a third wheel. And unless he's having car issues, I'm dead weight."

"But then you're able to see how he's doing?"

"There's an app for that." He grabbed his phone off the coffee table, and flipped it open, giving her a funny stare. "You should know there's an app for everything."

She glanced at his screen.

Lucas thumbed through the standings. "Later tonight, it'll show his times and placings. I'll show you."

Aurora gave him a half-hearted shrug. "Okay." But she wasn't sure if she actually wanted to see. "What if... What if he gets in an accident?"

It had happened before. Nate had been in a full head-on collision, which became part of the reason she broke up with him. Although he was fine, she'd watched it play out in person. It terrified her thinking she'd lost Nate the same way she'd lost her momma and sister.

"Then nothing shows up for his lap time."

"Oh." Her voice fell.

A knife scraped across a plate and Lucas winced.

"We can do something else. It's not as exciting to watch a tiny screen as it is to watch it live."

Says you.

She nodded.

"Anyway," Lucas said after swallowing a bite of pancake. "I'd prefer to do the something else as I have this plan for tonight. Something different and fun. And unexpected."

"Unexpected? Now my wheels are turning."

"Good."

She narrowed her eyes at him as a playful smile stretched across her face. "That's it? No hints."

"I've given you lots already."

"Yeah, different, fun and unexpected. Not much to work with." She studied the playful expression he displayed. "Is there a time I should be aware of?"

"Yeah, later." He laughed as he picked up his dishes and carried them into the kitchen.

"Rummy," Lucas said, fanning out a pair of sevens, and three nines.

"Damn you."

"And that's the game." He laughed, adding up his score. "You'll never beat me at cards."

"Yeah? Well it's an old person's game, anyway."

"That would be true if it wasn't me and you playing."

She gathered up the deck and fed them back into the case. "Where'd you learn to play?"

"My Pops. Used to play in the camper as kids out at the track. Claimed it was supposed to help us out think the other players, but it never did. All that happened was he'd kick our asses every game, but it never stopped us from trying to outsmart him. One day we vowed we'd win."

"Did you?"

"No, but there's still time." Lucas stood up and stretched out. "Speaking of time, is it six o'clock already?"

She craned her neck and checked the clock. Standing up, she peered out the patio doors. The sun was still fairly high up, pouring bright light into the living room and brightening up the kitchen. With the sun setting after nine pm, it was hard to pinpoint a set dinner time. Having supper when it got dark out only applied in the winter. She refocused her sights on him. "Are you getting hungry?"

"Actually, yes."

She walked into the kitchen, opening up the fridge. "I'll start dinner."

Lucas joined her, leaning over the top of the fridge. "I didn't say that so you would cook me dinner. I was thinking we'd go out tonight."

"I thought we were done with the driving today? My body can't handle any more, remember? That's why you started kicking my ass in cards."

"Yeah, I'm aware. You had enough blackouts this morning to last a lifetime." Strawberry-blond hairs stood on end as he ran his fingers through his hair. "We can walk. There are a couple of available options nearby."

She closed the fridge. "Sure, let's do that. I don't feel much like cooking anyways. I'll go freshen up." As she spun on her foot, a thought popped into her head, causing her to slam her other foot down. "Wait? Is this about that surprise?"

"No." He shook his head. "That comes later."

A tilt of her head. "Okay."

"Go clean up. I'll tidy up out here."

A few minutes later, with piqued curiosity, she emerged from her bedroom. Sporting a silky amethyst-coloured top matched with tan shorts, she said, "I'm ready."

It used to bother her having her accident scars visible, but somewhere over the summer, that modesty disappeared. In a way, it was freeing.

Lucas did a double take.

"I know, different right?" She waved her hand up and down. "I figure if we're going out for a dinner, and there's no training involved, I wanted to dress up a little."

"Now I'm under-dressed."

His camo green shorts and a grey t-shirt were totally acceptable.

"You look fine," she said. The apartment stood tall behind them, shrinking the further they walked away. "It's hard to believe summer is almost over."

"I know, right? It went by so fast."

"And when you start classes, you're taking…"

For a fraction of a second he hesitated in his footing.

"You still haven't told her? Lucas!"

He huffed as his shoulders slumped. "It's not that easy, okay? I've tried with her, and it always comes back to the money issue. If I do well overall in the season, maybe I'll have enough to set aside for the second term. But I'd be throwing away so much by doing that."

"That may be true," she kept time with him. "But think of all you'll be gaining? You have a real gift for reading people, and this isn't the first time I've mentioned it. There's something about you that instantly puts people at ease and makes them want to spill their darkest secrets."

"Oh ha ha."

"You know it's true. You and Chris could go into business together. Collectively you'd heal a lot of sick, twisted people."

A sad smile appeared, and he rubbed the back of his neck. "I haven't healed you."

"Maybe I'm not the right type."

"You mean there's a specific type of sick and twisted?" The arch of his eyebrow was high enough to touch his hairline.

"Yeah, and if you enrolled in psych you'd know that." A small giggle snuck out.

"Touché." He shoved his hands deep into his pockets. "There has to be something we're missing… September's a heartbeat away, and you're no where ready to make the trip there."

Tendrils of hair fell against her cheeks as she hung her head. "I know. Online classes are becoming more and more like a long-term reality. It sure would be nice to make it longer than five minutes before losing my mind."

"We'll get it figured out, there's got to be a solution. Something we haven't thought of."

They turned onto the sidewalk that led to UB's Sports Pub.

"It's like that old saying, *it was in the last place I looked.* Well, duh, only a special type of idiot would keep looking for something after they've already found it. That's the very definition of insanity."

He nodded and stopped to hold the door for her as they entered. Noisy chatter from dozens of customers happily replaced the normal assault of twangy music that ached her eardrums. All of whom were sitting at tables decorated with easels and plates of paint.

Lucas spoke up from behind her. "What's going on?" The giant smirk he tried to hide said it all. The bugger knew.

"Lucas," she said, glancing around. At the end of one of the tables at the back, she spotted someone familiar. "Kaitlyn?" As she sidestepped a waitress with a tray full of drinks, another face popped out from behind an easel. "Daddy?" Her eyes bugged out. "What's going on?" She rushed over to give her daddy a hug. "What are you doing here?"

Should I be worried? I have been keeping up with my daily calls.

"Painting a picture of buildings, apparently." He thumbed to a large picture hanging off the partition separating the bathrooms from the main area.

She cocked an eyebrow. "No, really?"

"Ask him."

Turning on the spot, she faced Lucas. "What's going on?"

"Surprise."

"What?"

Kaitlyn squeezed her hand. "We're celebrating your birthday."

"But, it's not until next week."

"Yeah, but this was the only night they were available," Lucas said, nodding at Kaitlyn and her father. "I told you we were gonna do something different, fun and unexpected."

"Oh my god," she said, her smile widened and her heart raced a little faster. "This really is totally unexpected."

Lucas beamed and walked over to her father. "Pleasure to finally meet you in person, Mr. MacIntyre. Thanks for coming."

"Anything for my Princess. And please call me Cole."

Lucas nodded as colour warmed his cheeks. "I'll try."

"You'll get used to it," Kaitlyn said, tapping Cole's arm. "He claims being called *Mr.* MacIntyre makes him sound old."

"Well, it does." Daddy sat back on his bar stool and took a long swig of his dark-coloured drink. "Not a beer…" he said in her direction. "It's a coke."

She shook her head gently as she raised her hands. "I didn't ask." Putting her foot on the stool, she hoisted herself up across from him.

Lucas sat on her left and Kaitlyn on her right.

She had to crane her neck, however, to see the painting. Her jaw dropped at the intricate colors and design.

"Anyone ever done this before? I'm sure I have no skills for this."

The instructor popped up behind her, his knit cap tightly encasing dark curls. "It's easy, at least, if I'm doing my job properly it should be. I'll walk around and check on you at each step." He patted her on the shoulder with long, spindly fingers. Each nail painted a different colour.

Lucas leaned closer to her. "Was he flirting with you?"

"I certainly hope not." She turned and searched the area, unable to find the instructor. "He's weird."

Kaitlyn chimed in. "All artists are."

With drinks in hand, the group followed the instructor as he explained how to paint the background.

"This isn't so hard," Aurora said as long strokes of blue streaked across the top of her canvas.

"Yeah right," Lucas said, frustration in his voice. "Holding a paintbrush is completely different than a socket wrench. It's making my fingers cramp."

Cole laughed beside him. "You need to learn to relax there, boy."

Boy? Really, Daddy.

"Yeah, well painting is a skill I don't possess."

Cole said, "Watch. You need to add a touch more water to your brush. Like this."

She had no idea what her daddy was doing, but a quick scan of Lucas' raised eyebrows and knowing nod meant he understood.

Kaitlyn leaned in real close and whispered, "They seem to get along pretty well, eh? Better than Nate ever did."

She eyed the men as they bantered back and forth. There was no tension between either man, and more than a few smiles. They really were getting along. Guess daddies don't like the boyfriends as much as they do the platonic friends.

When the conversation between Lucas and Cole turned to shop talk and tools, she ignored them both, and focused her attention to Kaitlyn. "What's the word on Tatiana?"

"Not much at the moment."

"Why? What's going on?"

An angry swipe of dark blue scratched across Kaitlyn's canvas. "There's an issue getting her papers in order."

Aurora dropped her paintbrush into the water. "Is she moving here?"

"Well, she can't if she doesn't get her ducks in a row. Right now, she'll get a visitor pass, but she'll have to go back home within a few months." Kaitlyn swiped her brush back and forth over the streak of blue. "As it is, she won't be here until just before Thanksgiving."

"Thanksgiving?" Her voice pitched. That was still a long time away.

Kaitlyn forced a smile. "Yeah, but at least I'll have something to be thankful for, and maybe even something to celebrate." Her perfectly-plucked eyebrow raised as she spoke. In following the instructor's prompt, she dabbled a mixture of dark grey onto the top corner. "Speaking of things you're thankful for, how's that list coming along?"

"Brutal. But we're working on it."

"We're?"

"Yeah, Lucas is helping. Quite a bit actually." Until it rolled off her tongue and a pained expression covered Kaitlyn's face, she hadn't thought much about what that meant. It was one friend helping another. "Why is him helping me so wrong?" Her voice was so low, she worried Kaitlyn didn't hear.

"It's not that it's wrong, it's just... I could've..." She hopped off her stool, and walked behind Cole, placing a hand on his shoulder. "Oh wow, I love what you did with the sky."

Damn. There was no way Kaitlyn was jealous of her and Lucas, was she? Yet, Kaitlyn stood behind Daddy, laying the compliments on a little thick. She didn't sneak a glance in her direction, and made no effort to see Lucas' painting either. What the hell was up with her?

PaintNite ended faster than Aurora would've liked. As she put the finishing touches of yellow windows on the black buildings, the instructor congratulated the group on a successful evening.

Aurora slipped off her stool and went to admire Kaitlyn's handiwork. She gave her shoulders a friendly squeeze. "It's truly wonderful, Kait."

Her hand landed on Aurora's. "Not bad for a first timer."

"No, not bad at all."

"Can we talk tomorrow? I don't want you to ever think–"

Kaitlyn turned toward her. "Yes. We'll do lunch?"

"Deal." She gave her friend a genuine smile and stepped over to Daddy's painting.

Her jaw hit the floor. It was stunning. The little details he added made the buildings come alive. The full moon had highlights and shadows, not just a white ball like hers was. The bridge in the foreground wasn't a simple-looking bridge either, but rather complex with ornate railings and towers.

"Geez, Daddy. Way to show us all up."

"What?" He shrugged. "It's okay?"

Lucas peeked his head over. "Wowsers, Mr— Cole. That's truly... wow."

"Oh, Cole," Kaitlyn said, touching his shoulder again. "It really is a masterpiece."

"Thanks, Kaitlyn," he said and signed his name to the bottom corner.

Aurora moved around her father to check out Lucas' work. He'd been struggling with his, and the instructor had stopped by several times to offer assistance. She stifled a gasp. Lucas had the artistic talents of a five-year-old, and that would be giving him credit. His buildings were tipped, and the little windows were not in a nice, neat line. The bridge did not appear to be strong enough to hold the two shadowed figures on it.

"What do you think?"

Her gaze drifted "I think… Well, I think it's a definite original."

"Good thing I drive better than I paint."

"Yes, good thing," Cole said, standing up. "That's my Princess you're carting around."

"And I value her life above my own, Sir."

Cole patted Lucas on the back. "Glad to hear that."

"Was tonight fun?" Lucas asked as they walked back to the apartment, each carrying a canvas.

Try as she may, she hadn't been able to wipe the smile off her face. "Totally."

"Any part specifically?"

She blinked and thought out loud, "The painting part was really neat. I had no idea they did anything like that. I loved hanging out with everyone. The food was really great. My cheeks hurt from laughing so much."

Lucas nudged into her. "I think you have a few more things to write down on your list."

"Thank you."

"For what?"

"You know…" Her hand waved through the air. "For putting this together. For making me forget about my problems for a while. I had a perfect evening."

"Good, I'm *happy* to hear that."

"Oh stop," she said, rubbing her shoulder into his arm.

❤ Chapter Nine ❤

The Happiness Project stared at her from the weathered table in the shrink's office. She was close, oh so close, to completing it. It had been four weeks since its inception. Four weeks of learning who she was, and what made her happy.

"Your list is getting better," Dr. Navin said. "A little less Miss America."

She was back in the tiny space, thinking out loud about her feelings. After a half-dozen appointments, she actually looked forward to seeing him. Although he was a tad patronizing, she appreciated the directness. There was something about him that made it easy for her to talk.

"Yep, just a few more things to write."

"I like the depth you are going with this. Have you learned anything about yourself in the process?"

She shifted in her seat, tucking her feet under her. "Surprisingly, yes."

"Care to share?"

"Why not?"

She ran her fingers over the remaining scabs on her chest tattoo. Joy filled her heart as her fingertips touched the tender tissue. The tattoo had been a total impulse, but she knew exactly what she wanted by the time her feet pulled her into the parlour. It didn't take long, but alone, the tears slipped out as the needles punctured her skin. Fifteen minutes later the words 'Tomorrow is never promised' were scrawled across her upper chest and shoulder in the most beautiful script.

"I am starting to appreciate everything in my life. To be thankful for my friends who have been instrumental in helping me this summer. I'm also grateful for my father. He and I weren't always close, but this summer, we've come a long way."

"Have you told him that?"

"Yes, several times." A tickling sensation danced out to her extremities. "I made it my daily project to write a thank you note. Ever read the book called '365 Thank Yous'?"

He shook his head.

"This guy wrote a letter every day to someone who touched him in some way. It was so inspirational, I've adopted it. Now I send a thank you note every day."

"Wow. I must say I'm impressed."

"Thank you." Pride rose in her.

"And what brought on this change?"

She shook her head. "I don't know really. The fifty things list maybe. I can't answer that."

"Well, be grateful then for wherever it came from." He ran his hand down his leg. "How have the training sessions with Lucas been going?"

The room brightened as she spoke. "We finally had a breakthrough."

Dr. Navin leaned in.

"Remember, how that five-minute point was literally the breaking point? How my body blacked out at that moment, every single time?" Her words poured forth at a breakneck speed.

He nodded in confirmation. "Yes, that's been troubling you both."

"Lucas figured it out."

"Did he now?"

"Yes. Simple really, I don't know why no one thought of it before. No offense."

His eyes widened at the comment. "I don't know why you think you'd offend me."

"Because even you didn't clue in."

"Well, now I'm curious."

She huffed. "One day after training, after *another* black out, we're parked in the Safeway parking lot. Lucas asked a few questions about the accident. All totally innocent, just trying to get more information. Well, that night, he took off for a while and when he came home, he was lit up like a Christmas Tree."

"Why?"

"Because he figured it out. He went to the accident scene and backtracked to the spot where Carmen handed me the keys to her car." Her hands flew all over as she spoke. "He drove from the restaurant we ate at to the scene. Do you know what? That distance was five minutes and four seconds. Can you believe it?"

Dr. Navin sat in silence.

"Since we had, well Lucas had, figured out why I was blacking out at that specific time—when the crash happened–"

"Slow down, you lost me back there."

She was so proud to share this information, she felt like sunshine emitted from her pores.

"Okay." She took a deep breath. "When Lucas discovered the connection between the black out time and the accident, he worked to figure out a way to get past it." She took another breath to stop herself from rambling. "And it worked! We finally broke through the five-minute barrier."

A skeptical expression complete with raised brows and a puckered forehead decorated his face. "How?"

"It's kind of silly really."

He leaned much closer, fixated on her.

"I hold this necklace in my right hand, and Lucas holds my left hand." She pulled out a silver anchor charm with a cross and heart on it from her pocket. Nate had given it to her as a gift. Heat filled her cheeks. "And I…"

Sheesh, it sounded so much better when it was just me and Lucas. Her mouth dried out, and her pulse sped up. In a whispered voice, she said, "I say over and over *It's not my fault, it's not my fault.*"

Dr. Navin rubbed his chin in deep thought, and remained expressionless. Leaning back into his couch, he inhaled and exhaled. Twice.

Say something. Please. Anything.

"And that works?"

She swallowed. "Both times we tried it, yes. Even managed to make it to ten minutes."

He thrust himself forward again. "Why'd you stop there?"

"Because the images start to close in. However, once we stop, they fade away." She shrugged.

"Interesting."

Seconds ticked by. Heartbeats passed. Breaths were breathed. The wait to hear more from him ate her up inside. He remained speechless, blankly staring at the wall. What he was doing, she didn't know. He rubbed his thumb across the notepad. She picked at her nails, and tore off a hangnail, turning her fingertip a bright crimson red.

Unable to take it anymore, she flat out asked, "Dr. Navin, did we do something wrong?"

He shook his head quickly. "No, you didn't. I've just never heard of something like that working. It's not wrong, because it worked. However, I would like to confer with my colleagues on this, and get their opinion. It's very interesting to me because I know how much you blame yourself for what happened."

She did. At least until a couple of days ago. It had been hard, but to say it out loud was to believe it. And a month ago she would've never believed the accident wasn't her fault. After all, she *was* the driver and their safety and responsibility rested on her shoulders.

He shook his head. "When's our next appointment?"

"Friday."

"Great. That gives me some time."

"Dr. Navin, I'm worried, and you're making me freak out just a little bit."

He scooted further to the edge of the couch and put the note pad filled with blue writing within sight. "Aurora, the mind is an incredible machine. We haven't even begun to figure out all the complexities of it. What works for one person exhibiting the same symptoms, fears and rationalizations, will not always work on the next. Many times it's a matter of trial and error until we find a solution that solves the problem. And sometimes the solution presents itself in such a way, it's a wonder it wasn't seen before." He clasped his hands together. "Does that make sense?"

The corner of her mouth curled up. "A little, I suppose."

"Who came up with the idea?"

"Lucas, but he said he had help."

A small snort came from Dr. Navin, followed quickly by a grin. "No doubt, Dr. Johnson had a hand in it. That woman has some unique ideas."

She couldn't help herself; a smile burst through. "She really does."

Like the time she thought giving her some sleeping pills would make a trip home from the track achievable. She shook the horrible memory away.

"I want you and Lucas to continue doing what you're doing. It's working, and it's got you to a point you never thought you'd be at again."

This was all truth.

"Are you back in school?"

She nodded. "Starting Thursday."

"Will Lucas be driving you?"

"The drive time is still a little far, but we'll be there before long I'm sure."

For once, she believed it would happen. She really believed it.

"Any relapses?"

"Would I be here if there were? Don't you think I'd skip out?"

"Actually, I don't think you would. Not anymore."

Hmph. Shows you what you know. This would be the last place I'd be.

He brushed down his pants as he rose. "Is there anything further you'd like to discuss?"

"Not that I can think of."

"Well, I look forward to discussing this with you on Friday. Good luck with your first day."

Thankful the appointment was over, she stood and gave her hip a quick rub.

He gave her a quick once-over. "Everything okay?" He walked to the door with her file in his chubby hand.

"Yes. It gets stiff when I don't move it enough." She met his gaze head on. "It's all good. I can work through it, *non*-medically." Like a volcano spewing lava, pride poured out of her. If anyone had told her six months ago, she'd been reaching this point, she would've laughed in their face. The power of believing anything is possible if you believe in yourself has changed her in more than a handful of ways. The best part, she wasn't alone on this journey. Her strongest cheerleaders walked beside her.

❤ Chapter Ten ❤

The calendar loomed large in front of her, the big reveal date circled in red. So much to accomplish in only two weeks. So much *had* been accomplished already. She was quite proud of what she could now do and knew she wouldn't be where she was without the Johnsons. Nate started her out and Lucas was finishing it up, and somewhere in the middle, Chris was fine-tuning the process. Bless them all for contributing their piece to the puzzle.

All the hard work gave her a tentative hope. If Nate was still dating Marissa, would he be pleased to see her? Would he drop Marissa like a hot potato and welcome her back with open arms? Or would she walk away from the track heartbroken and disappointed? At the start of the summer she'd set out a goal to win him back and conquer her fears but that plan never included him dating someone else.

Two weeks. Two weeks until—if nothing else—she could see him in person. His brown hair, those chocolate-coloured eyes, that dreamy, lopsided smile that warmed her right to her core… Oh, how her heart ached and missed his touch. It had become her new drug, and she craved it.

"Hey," Lucas said, interrupting her brooding.

"Hey." She removed her gaze from the calendar.

"You okay?"

"Totally." She forced a smile as he placed a cup of coffee in her hand.

He took a long drink from his mug. "I need to leave you alone for a bit today."

"Thank god," she said in jest, smiling at him. "I thought you'd never leave."

In truth though, except for Saturday nights when he was at the track, he hadn't left her alone for more than a few of hours since the Benedryl moment. No matter where he was, he checked in. To make sure she was okay and wasn't up to anything that would be a detriment to their plans. She knew she was being watched, and rightfully so. She'd earned it and in a small way, it warmed her heart to know he cared.

"But I have an idea for tonight. It's been school-school-work-work all week. Time to kick back a little bit because my brain is completely fried."

She stared at him, wondering what he was dreaming up in that head of his. "Fun sounds good. Like real fun—not car crash video fun or anything like that."

The thought of a night of dancing at Urban DC lit her up. She hadn't been out to let loose in a long time. Her hip had improved enough over the summer with the incessant physio, she wouldn't even need a drug to prevent any pain from showing up. Not that she had any percs anyways.

"Good." He raised his mug in the air. "We're gonna attempt a longer drive though."

"I thought you said we were going to kick back a little? A long drive sounds like work." She cocked an eyebrow at him and tipped her head to the side.

"Nothing I think you can't handle."

"That's a double negative."

"Anyway," he said and leaned against the wall while she sat at the table. "I've been thinking. For the journey to the track, it's over forty-five minutes. Now, clearly, we've finally broken that nasty five-minute mark." A large grin spread across his face, lighting up his grey-blues when he spoke. "We're making excellent progress but there's no way you'll make that length of trip in one shot, so I plan on breaking it up into smaller segments."

"Like how? Take a week to get down there?"

"Yeah, because that's not impractical at all." He gulped down the coffee. "I'm gonna break the trip up into manageable fifteen minute drives. I think that's within reach."

80

"Barring no traffic."

"Of course. Then, plan for lots of break time at each stop. Figure that way, it should be easier."

"Our break time will likely be longer than the drive time."

He shrugged. "So be it. I'll plan accordingly. We'll leave here at three or something, maybe even earlier."

She sighed and thought about it.

It would *make it easier. And we're close to the fifteen-minute drive time, being that we're at ten minutes now. By the end of next week, fifteen should be doable. Totally. It's a long time, but with some healthy breaks...*

"You know, it just may work."

"Excellent," he said. "We'll do a dry run on a much smaller scale tonight, if you're game."

"If I'm game? Hmm, I may have to check my schedule. I don't know if there's much room in there for long drawn-out fun."

"I'm pretty sure your evening's free and clear."

"Yes, but my afternoon is full. Physio at one, shrink at two."

"Well, that'll give you time to unwind and relax as I'll be back at eight to pick you up."

"I look forward to whatever you have planned." She saw the excitement dancing in his eyes and quickly refocused on her coffee. "Or maybe not."

Butterflies swarmed in her belly. Three long, successive trips. Each longer than she'd done before. Her chest tightened at the thought of it. What if she couldn't do it?

A quick glance to him. He still smiled at her.

He swatted her shoulder playfully. "Stop worrying. It'll be fun."

"I'll have to believe you. For now."

"A date at eight."

"Don't be late." She smirked, the tightness in her chest easing.

"Never."

As promised, Lucas knocked on her door at eight p.m. He walked in all cleaned up in a nice pair of jeans and a ST. FX shirt.

Sitting in the living room, she lifted her nose to the air. "Oh my god. I smell orange. What are you hiding?"

A sheepish grin played on his face as he sauntered over. "You can smell that?"

"I can," she said. The scent of orange mixed with another floral scent.

Lucas pulled out a bouquet from behind his back. "I didn't think you'd be able to smell these."

A small gasp came from her as she noticed a flower with white petals. "Are those mock orange?"

She stood and buried her nose into the blooms, deeply inhaling the scent. With it came a flood of emotions. She was seven or eight, and remembered sitting in the best spot on the front porch where if the breeze blew just right, she would be covered in the orange smell—fragrant without being overpowering. "Wherever did you?"

"It wasn't hard. I called around to a few greenhouses and picked up a few branches. They kinda thought it was weird." The wrapped flowers were pushed into her hands. "The others are–"

"Stargazer lilies, white roses and hyacinth."

"Wow," he said. "You know your flowers."

Holding them under her nose, she breathed in the scent as she walked to the kitchen. She hunted for a vase from the back of a cupboard and filled it with tepid water. A quick unwrap and she tenderly added the flowers, sniffing in the memories again.

"They're really beautiful," she said.

"I'm glad you like them. You mentioned loving an orange smelling plant."

Her heart swelled. "Thank you for remembering."

It surprised her that he remembered, but then again, it didn't. Not considering everything he'd done.

"So you'll be happy to know, I checked in with mom today." He shifted from foot to foot. "Even had dinner with her."

The confidence he'd had moments ago flittered away as he fidgeted like a boy in a trouble.

"What's with the hesitation?" she asked.

"Well…"

"She brought it up again, didn't she?"

Lucas nodded.

Her hands landed on her hips. "And you cowered, right? Didn't stand up for yourself and tell her how much you're hating engineering and how you'd rather be in psychology? How you have a natural gift for sensing people's emotions? When are you going to tell her? When you graduate?"

"It's complicated. As much as I'd like to tell her off, I can't. It's disrespectful, and I was raised better than that." He bit his top lip and refused to make eye contact with her.

"You need to tell her," Aurora said, throwing her hands up in the air. "It's not going to get better or any easier."

He turned away from her and paced the length of the living room. "I know, I know, but tonight wasn't the right night."

"Why?" She interrupted his walk and stood in front of him. No way was he going to shirk away from telling his mom. If he needed someone in his corner, she was going to back him one hundred percent.

"Bill was there."

"Bill?"

"The track owner." Lucas rolled his eyes. "Apparently, they're pretty serious."

A high-pitched gasp escaped her. "How serious? Like could he be your step-dad?"

His shiver made her laugh.

"Maybe. I hope not, but maybe."

"Isn't that a conflict of interest?"

"No more than Nate dating Marissa." Disgust rang through his voice.

Ugh.

A lightbulb went off, and her heart plummeted. "They were there tonight too, weren't they? I thought they'd all be out at the track? It *is* Friday."

He dismissed her first question with a wave. "We'll go early tomorrow morning. Nate needs to fix something under the beast, and it's easier here where there's a lift. Are you ready to go?" He checked the time on his watch.

"Stop hiding it. Tell me. She was there, wasn't she?"

"What difference does it make?" He walked through the eating area, over to the door.

She balanced her weight on her left foot. Her right hip was still sore from a gruelling round of physio that afternoon. "If they're serious, then this big plan of mine is going to fail epically. What am I supposed to do? Show up at the track and beg him to dump the bitch and choose me instead?"

"I'm pretty sure it won't last." He opened the door. "C'mon. We need to get going."

"The plan? Or those two?"

He cocked an eyebrow.

"How can you be so sure *now*? You've been saying that for weeks."

"Something about the way he kept brushing her off tonight. He seemed on edge."

Sounds like everyone was on edge. Must've been a helluva supper.

Lucas interrupted her thoughts. "Hey, we can hope for the best."

"That they break up?"

"That's the hope. She's such an evil bitch. Nate had it so much better with you." He winked. "Now come on, let's go. I have a plan to put into motion. Timing is crucial."

Raw fear coursed through her bones. Lucas wore his excitement like a florescent shirt, bright enough for all to see and blinded by. She only wished she could mirror that. The only part of tonight she prepared for was the drive. Everything else was a complete mystery. And that was nothing to get super excited about.

That mystery danced in Lucas' mischievous expression. "Let's go," he said

She followed him out, shaking her foot as she locked the door.

"Why are you limping so much?" he asked.

"Rough physio today."

"Are you hurting?"

"Aching more than hurting. But it's manageable." Instinctively she gave her hip a rub. "They offered me an Advil, but I refused it."

Lucas spun on the spot. "You did?" A huge smile sprang up from ear to ear. Pride poured out of him in the sweetest tone. "That's really great news."

"I'm trying. But it's like they've been in cahoots with my shrink—the pain is a reminder that I'm alive. What a joke."

The elevator chimed, and they stepped in. Lucas hit the down button as she braced herself against the wall. That first little drop did little to quell the butterflies. What were they going to do between drives? Curiosity gnawed on her.

"Well, let me know if it starts aching," he said.

"Are you planning on making me run somewhere?"

He laughed. "No, not at all."

"Whew, because that would be difficult."

"Only because you've never done it."

One point to Lucas.

The sun hung in the western sky as she and Lucas walked to the car. Lengthy shadows cascaded over the building with slight flickers of gold glinting off windows. The heat of the day surrounded them in a comfortable warmth–for now. The cool autumn night was fast approaching. Lucas tossed her coat into the backseat.

Foot firmly in place, she shook out her hands, trying to mentally prepare herself for the unknown. "So what's the plan? What do I need to brace myself for?"

"Simple. We're gonna take a long ride–"

Her eyes opened so wide she should've been concerned they'd fall out, but it was the least of her worries.

"According to Google maps, it's ten minutes to the first destination. It's not a busy time of day, so we should be right on schedule." He opened the passenger door.

"First destination?"

"Yeah, remember, I said this would be a test run for the long trip to the track."

She paced the length of the car shadow. "I remember, was just hoping you'd forgotten. Are we headed to the track?"

"Guess you'll have to find out."

It was the smirk that charmed her. She could do this. Baby steps. Sadness clouded her heart.

Baby steps...

It's what Nate called his training program with her—Operation Baby Steps. Briefly, she wondered if he were near. Could he see her progress? He'd be so stoked. She glanced back at the car and over to Lucas.

This would be manageable right? She could do this easily. Three trips? Maybe not so much.

Think about it as a final test... If you can do this, you pass. Think about the end goal.

Lucas squeezed her shoulder, bringing her out of her mind and back into the present. "I promise, everything will be fine. Look inside on the dash."

She cocked her head to check it out. "What's that?" An ordinary piece of paper was taped to the dash.

"You can read it on the way." He rested his elbow on the top of the door frame. "Something to keep part of your focus on something other than the many fabulous accomplishments you're making."

Oh Lucas.

"Thanks." She stepped back and straightened herself out. "Oh, before I forget..." She thrust her hand deep into her pocket and pulled out a hastily wrapped package. "For you."

A wide grin spread from ear to ear as he ripped the wrapping off like a kid expecting to find a puppy. A puppy couldn't fit in the small box, but his face lit up as he pulled out the racing flag keychain. He flipped it over, tilting it to read the inscription. "Never drive faster than your guardian angel can fly."

She smiled up at him. "It's important to me that you stay safe. I'd hate to lose you—or anyone else for that matter—in a car crash."

He wrapped his arms around her and gave her a squeeze. "Thank you. It's perfect." He let go of her and attached it to his keys. "Ready to go?"

She swallowed the lump in her throat as she examined the car. Just metal and mechanics. Her ponytail swayed with the nod.

He leaned against the door. "Whenever you're ready."

"You should know, I'm never truly ready." She forced a smile. "But here goes nothing."

Huffing and puffing, she lowered herself into his car and reached for the seatbelt. It clicked into place, and she gave him the thumbs up sign. The door shut beside her, and Lucas got in the driver's seat. The car revved to life, and she placed her full trust in Lucas *and* his guardian angel.

Aurora quickly read the passage Lucas had taped to the dash. It was a long passage on hope and never giving up, however, it wasn't long enough to keep her attention. Taking a deep breath, she glanced out the window. "Where are we?"

"About to cross the river."

She no longer needed his hand, but reached for it regardless.

All previous drives had been on the main city streets, and never ever on the freeway. Even though she understood they'd need to travel on the highway to get the track, it made her jumpy seeing the trees whoosh by them in a dark green blur. It gave her a headache trying to focus on them. They sped down a slight embankment, where a long bridge spanned the distance in front of them

The bridge was long, or seemed that way, but the break from the blurry trees lent itself to a gorgeous view of the rushing river and endless banks of greenery lining either edge.

"It's so pretty," she said in a quiet voice, unable to tear her gaze away.

"Ever been here?"

"Not in recent years. Not that I remember anyways."

The drive over the water was quick, and before she knew it they were already climbing up the hill on the south end of the bridge.

"We're almost there," Lucas said, but his voice seemed far away.

Allowing the world to temporarily darken, she closed her eyes. She leaned against the head-rest clenching her fists as she tried to keep the image of the river in the forefront of her mind.

Focus on the trees. The brown of the river.

Lucas' rough hand covered her fists. "You're doing great."

Her breathing rate accelerated, and the back of her neck started sweating. Fingernails drove deep into the heels of her palms, but the pain didn't bother her. It never did.

Lucas gave her hand a gentle squeeze. "Nearly there. Keep breathing."

The car slowed and made a lazy right turn. A left turn, a right turn and another left before the vehicle slowed and came to a stop.

"We're here." He got out and raced to the passenger side.

When the door opened, she ejected herself from the car and stood five feet from it. She took deep breaths, shaking out her hands and kicking with her feet. "Where are we?"

"Overlooking the river. The sun's about to set. Apparently, according to my Twitter connections, this is a great spot to watch it go down. Or one of them. The absolute best spot is about a twenty-minute drive from the apartment. We're not there yet."

The view was a sight to behold. They stood on a sidewalk, the edge of a cliff just a few feet ahead of them where tall, ugly weeds flourished. The river was far below, silently winding and weaving its way between thick groves of trees and lush emerald-greenery. A warm, gentle breeze caressed her cheeks, causing her to revel in the sensation. The distant hum of a lawnmower was the only sound, but it brought with it the weak scent of freshly cut grass. There was something refreshing about that smell.

"Could you imagine living here?" she asked in a whisper, afraid any sound louder would destroy the serenity.

Three houses stood tall behind them.

She pointed to her right. "What a backyard view those people have. Imagine having an evening coffee there."

A house stood about fifty feet away. A lonely tree stood on the wrong side of the fence. It seemed to belong to… nothing. And somehow she understood its loneliness. Close enough to be part of the landscape beside it, yet separated.

Lucas followed her gaze. "Ah yes. Years ago, along this chunk of land, there used to be three houses, but the cliff gave way and they fell into the river. If you look, you can see the edges of the driveways."

She took a giant step back towards his car.

He laughed. "It was years ago. Like twenty or more years."

"And you brought me here why?"

His head cocked toward the west, and a long finger covered her lips. "Shh." He refocused his gaze to the west. "That's why."

Following his lead—hesitantly—she lifted herself up and sat beside him on the hood of his car. In the western sky, the blazing ball of yellowness hovered above the horizon casting its glow onto the scattered clouds. As his face was warmed by the streams of ambers and oranges, she couldn't help but stare at him. The bright rays of golden sun highlighted his strawberry-blond hair with subtle hues of bronze. The brilliance lasted a few seconds, but long enough to hold her undivided attention.

"You're not watching," he whispered, breaking the spell.

Her attention turned to the setting sun—an orb of brilliance that didn't hurt to stare at—the bottom portion of it already dipped below the tree line. All around the clouds reflected back streams of pinks, golden hues of yellow and the embers of a warm fire danced across the sky. It didn't take long for the sky to change, and the pinks to fade into the mauves of twilight. The fading glow from the sun lost its lustre as it fell beneath the horizon.

"Wow," she breathed, unable to find a better word. The whole event took less than five minutes, but it was the most incredible five minutes she'd spent in a long time. "That was… Wow."

He leaned close, their shoulders rubbing together. "I know, right?"

"Why'd you bring me here?"

Even in the dim of twilight she noticed his cheeks fill with colour. "I wanted you to remember why you used to love sunsets. You said it was something you used to enjoy. In the before times."

Yes, in the before times. Since then, she really hadn't given it much thought. But maybe that was because the drugs she took erased any notion of wanting to find something pretty to watch for a while.

"One other thing," he said as he hopped off the hood and reached inside the car. Taylor Swift began to play on the stereo. "Now, it goes against my better judgement to have this playing from my car..." He extended his hand as the melody sounded. "But may I have this dance anyway?"

A small part of her hesitated, but a larger part of her jumped at the chance.

She loved dancing.

So what if it was with Lucas?

After a sunset.

Beside a cliff-side scenic view.

Harmless, right? All day long she'd been hoping they'd go dancing, and here they were. Yeah, it wasn't the bar, but still. She placed her hand in his and shuffled her feet. The music filled her soul as soon as she let it in. It had been too long.

The melody moved her and took over, making her movements instinctual and purposeful.

"You're good at this."

"I know." She smiled, but had to admit, Lucas wasn't half bad either. A little stiff, but with time, he'd be a decent lead.

One song played, then another. Peels of giggles and laughter mixed in with the chords. A slow song danced out of the speakers, and she spun herself into him, pulling him close. He responded by moving his arm from her shoulder to the small of her back as she lay her head on his chest.

"This is perfect," his low voice rumbled.

His words broke the spell the music held over her.

Perfect?

Oh my god. This was wrong. The whole thing was wrong. She's not supposed to be with Lucas, dancing in the twilight beside a car.

No.

No.

No.

Her head shook. She stepped away from the embrace and wrapped her arms around her chest.

His expression changed and with it, his smile fell to the ground. "What's wrong?"

"Umm..." Another step back. "I... I... can't..."

"Aurora, you're scaring me just a bit. What's wrong?" His face was tight with concern.

She glanced up to him. "I can't..." Her grip tightened around her chest. "It's wrong." A quick breath. "Being here. Watching the sunset with you. Dancing with you in the twilight. It feels more than just a friendship."

"Oh." He stood there, but lowered his gaze. "I swear this is just a friendship."

Maybe her suspicions were correct. Shoulders rounded, he slumped against his car. The confident demeanour he held a moment ago disappeared in a flash.

"I'd like to go home please."

Nervously she opened her door, but she wasn't getting in until he at least made a move. No way was she going to sit in there any longer than need be. Didn't matter what was going on. Or not going on. Lucas continued to stand there, forlorn yet adorable.

"Please."

"Okay." He held her door and waited, patiently as always, for her to click herself into the car. "Did you want to go to the next stop?"

"No. I want to go home. Please. I need to go home."

The ride back home, although faster with less traffic, felt longer. Infinitely longer. The air between them was thick and uncomfortable. Neither spoke, and if he glanced her way, she never knew. Her hands stayed tightly clasped together and her focus was on the underside of her eyelids, wishing herself anywhere but where she was.

Aurora knew when they arrived home. The engine stopped and the cool night air slapped across her body. She shivered from the cold as she exited, but it wasn't just the air temperature.

An impatient huff sounded beside her. "Well…" He held up her jacket. "This is yours."

Standing beside the car, she didn't know what to say. Nothing seemed right. Everything would've been forced.

"Well, thanks for bringing me home." She sighed and shuffled. It was impossibly hard to look at him.

"As if I'd leave you there." He scratched his stubble-covered jaw and dropped his hands to his sides.

"Yeah," she said, avoiding his gaze. "I know you'd never do that."

He gestured to the front of the building and pushed his hair off his forehead. "I'll walk you up."

"I promise you, I'm good." She took a step back separating them further. "I'm sorry… you'll need to stay at your own house. I can't…"

A few more steps, and she turned her back to him.

This is too painful.

"Aurora," he called out as her feet touched the sidewalk leading to the main doors.

She spun around, slowly, carefully, fighting hard to stay standing on legs that wanted to collapse beneath her. She tried in earnest to hide her quivering chin.

He crossed the distance between them in a few long strides. "Please, I meant nothing romantic by tonight. Just two friends out having a good time."

"I'm in love with your brother."

"I know."

"And I get what you're trying to do, to make me see the fun in life, but it felt like a line was crossed."

"Was it the dancing?" His expression morphed into curiosity. A smile wanted to sneak out, but he used amazing restraint to keep it in check.

She crossed her arms over her chest. "Maybe. Maybe it was the whole thing. I don't know."

A rock on the ground became her focus. She kicked it across the parking lot.

"I know what you're thinking. I can read you, remember?"

The words froze her to the spot and her vision blurred.

"My only plan for tonight was to show you that there's life and fun away from the safety of your backyard."

She stepped backwards, inching closer to the door. Admittedly, she did have fun. For a moment she forgot who she was and what she battled. For a moment, she was no longer lost.

"There's something you need to know. Before I met you, I was a guy who spent all his time with a wrench in his hands, hanging out with other grease monkeys. Sure, I have friends, but now I know they're superficial. They never cared about me the way you do. It was always how best I can help them. But you... you've brought out a side in me I didn't know existed. I feel different around you—free—and I love that I can trust you with my secrets. You've given me a purpose. I love helping you, watching you learn and tackle your fears. It's the reason I want to change studies."

She wiped the tears with the side of her hand. "I have to go."

"Before you go, know this. Yes, I love you, but I'm not in love with you. I love you like a sister…" He paused and sighed. "Except I get along with you. I enjoy your company and I want this whole summer thing to work out for you and Nate. I'd never try to put the moves on you and take any chance of ruining our friendship. You mean far too much to me. You're my best friend, Aurora."

Tears fell hard and fast. Her head resembled a tornado of emotions, and she was unable to pick just one. He declared his love— for their friendship—and it made her heart ache. Tonight had been a perfect escape until it went too far. What the hell was going on?

Her body vibrated with the mixed feelings. Unsure of what to do, she backed up further. It was too much. It was all too much.

"Please, Aurora." His voice was raw as he pleaded with her.

"I'm sorry, I just need some time."

He took a step forward.

She thrust a hand up. "I'm sorry." She spun on her heel and headed into the building's foyer.

❤ Chapter Eleven ❤

"How can you be in love with him?" Kaitlyn said, passing Aurora a personal sized container of ice cream as she entered the apartment. "How is that even possible?" Her tone lacked warmth. It was downright condescending.

Aurora slumped onto the weathered couch and glanced around. The apartment felt different. Empty. Lonely. The picture of her and Nate lay flat on the shelf. She couldn't bear to have him staring at her. It was like he knew what had happened tonight.

A cool breeze blew in through the open patio door, the evening ripe with the city smell of rusting leaves and crisp air. Even from the 19th floor, revving engines and honking horns sounded in the distance.

She sighed. Maybe calling Kaitlyn had been a bad idea. She wanted comfort not a lecture.

A drawer in the kitchen banged shut, and Kaitlyn fell beside her, a spoon extended out in offering.

"Thanks."

Kaitlyn twisted in her spot. "No, really, how can you be in love with him?"

"I don't know, Kait. But it freaked me out when it dawned on me."

"So you blamed him?"

"Well, not really. We were dancing, and he whispered it was perfect. It cemented or verified or ugh, I don't know the word I'm looking for, but it hit me like a bolt of lightning."

Kaitlyn waved her spoon around. "This really complicates things."

"Tell me about it."

"So what are you going to do about it?"

Aurora scooped a taste of ice cream onto the spoon. "I need to figure this out. I don't want things to be awkward between us."

"Too late." Kaitlyn's tone was sarcastic but the truth was out there.

"I mean I don't want them to be more awkward."

"Yeah? Let me know how that works out." She gave her best motherly look. It always came with a side of guilt.

"Kaitlyn," she said quietly, casting her gaze downwards and avoiding eye contact.

"Are you sure it's love though? Maybe you're just lonely."

"I am lonely, but not in the sense of being alone, I–"

"I know what you're saying, that's why I suggested it. You miss Nate so much you're transferring your feelings to Lucas."

With a shake of her head and a long blink, she said, "That doesn't make any sense at all."

Kaitlyn put her ice cream container on the side table. "Of course it does. You and Lucas have been together every day since when? July? Or at least almost every day. He's helping you through some really tough shit, and you are depending on him. You've never depended on anyone, and I should know. I was your best friend first." She bit her bottom lip almost as though she was trying to stop the quivering. Her arms retracted closer to her body as her shoulders rolled inwards.

"But I…"

Kaitlyn sighed and pushed away from her. "It's okay to depend on someone. It doesn't make you weak. I promise. In fact, I'm glad you depend on him, it means he's earned your trust."

She stared at her friend. Kaitlyn could be summed up in five words: older, wiser and always right. A sister from another momma.

"But they're so different," Aurora said. "Nate and Lucas."

"Not as different as you think." Kaitlyn twisted the spoon in the ice cream. "They share a lot of similar mannerisms. Enough that even I picked up on it."

"You didn't know Nate."

"That may be slightly true, but I know what he did to you, for you. Lucas has that in spades. You're more confident. You're more cheerful. Your determination to beat this thing never ends."

A drop of ice cream fell onto her necklace charm, and she gave it a lick. "What does that have to do with Lucas?" Her tongue ran over her lips.

"Because he brought it out of you. Just like Nate did."

She rolled her eyes. "So?" The spoon scrapped across the bottom of the container. Empty already? Damn tiny containers. She could eat a litre of ice cream, maybe more. Needed to swallow away her guilt.

"So?" Kaitlyn snickered. "It's like they're the same person but not. Lucas is younger, much closer to your age. Nate's my age."

"Age doesn't mean anything. You and Tatiana are seven years apart."

She waved away the comment with her spoon. "You and Lucas…" She inhaled and blew out her breath. "Do I dare say it?"

"Spit it out."

"You two have bonded. A lot. And very deeply, I might add. It's more than just physical. You've bonded on a mental and emotional level. Some would argue that's much stronger. And it's only natural that your feelings for Nate transferred to Lucas."

"I haven't transferred anything to anyone." Aurora rose and tossed the empty containers into the garbage. "If Nate were to be on the other side of that door when I opened it, I'd jump into his arms."

"What if they were both there?" Kaitlyn cocked an eyebrow and pointed.

She whipped her head toward the door as if expecting to see them both.

"There's your answer."

"What? I didn't even answer."

"Precisely."

No!

The need to stand and put distance between Kaitlyn and her honesty washed over her.

I love Nate and I've missed every single day that I could've–should've–been with him.

She stepped towards the patio door and searched the parking lot. Lucas' car was noticeably absent.

No, my heart belongs to Nate. But what about Lucas? What will become of us when I get back with Nate? Will he still come around?

The thought of him suddenly vanishing from her life frightened her.

She needed to walk. Back and forth she paced, looping between the living room and kitchen. It felt good, the movement was necessary. Deep within her soul, the rumblings of a panic attack built.

Walk it off. Keep going. Shake it off.

She paced the tiny length of her galley kitchen. Back and forth.

Kaitlyn's voice broke through her thoughts. "Aurora?"

She tried to brush her off. "Give me a minute."

"What's going on?"

"I'm trying to prevent a panic attack."

She touched Aurora's arm. "What can I do?"

"Nothing." She removed Kait's hand. Her touch wasn't the comfort Aurora wanted, or craved, or needed.

Oh, geez I really am falling for him.

"Just give me space."

Kaitlyn stepped to the side, her glare piercing as she walked past.

Aurora shook her hands as if trying to shake away the energy building. Her heart raced, her breathing quickened.

Lucas. Lucas would know how to calm me. But I need to stop depending on that. I need to do this on my own. I need to focus on something else. The Xanax. I have one. Somewhere.

Needing to dispense the energy, she made her way down the hall.

She searched through her bathroom. Through her bedroom. Under stacks of papers. On top of piles of clothes.

"Where the hell is it?"

The search continued in the main bathroom as cupboard doors opened and slammed shut. There had to be one little pill left. Out in the main area, she dumped the contents of her purse in hopes of uncovering the container. Nothing.

Fuck!

Lucas would probably have all the answers. He'd know what to do.

But I can't call him. I can do this on my own. Where's the fucking pill?

Speed walking back and forth between the bathroom and kitchen, she continued her endless search. Papers went flying. Drawers banged. Fists smacked countertops.

In frustration, Aurora collapsed on the floor in the kitchen. Kaitlyn dropped down, pulling Aurora into her arms.

"I need my pills. I don't want to feel anymore. I can't do this." Arms tightened around her, holding her together. "I need something to take away the anxiety. The pain of thinking I'm falling for someone I shouldn't be. I'm hurting the ones I love. If I wasn't–" *here anymore…* The idea of vocalizing that thought would scare her best friend, so she kept mum.

Kaitlyn silently brushed her fingers through Aurora's hair, each downward motion more soothing than the one before.

"Why can't I have my pills? I'd give anything for one. Just one little pill to make it all better."

"That's not what you need."

A loud sob poured from her. "But it is. I can't live without them. It's impossible. I need more than I'm given."

Now she wished she'd kept the Advil from physio, maybe that would take the edge off. Probably not. But she'd never know. And wanting—needing—to take another pain killer made the sob stronger and louder. "I don't want to do this anymore. I can't keep fighting this."

Kaitlyn held her as tightly as she could. "We'll get through this."

"I'll never be anything more than this. It's not worth it. It's too hard." Pushing out of her friend's arms, she sagged against the wall. "I'm not worth it."

"But you are. You just need to have your pity party and then you'll be okay."

It wasn't a pity party she was having. She knew the dark road her thoughts were about to turn onto. Having travelled them once before, she remembered the darkness. The easy way out. Right now, she wanted someone who understood what she was going through and sadly, neither Kaitlyn nor Lucas really understood that.

She reached into her pocket and pulled out her phone. Her head flopped against the wall. "Chris. I need help. Badly."

Thirty minutes later Chris, the twenty-nine-year-old shrink who looked closer to forty with the tight lines on her forehead and creases surrounding her eyes, slumped into the nearby kitchen chair.

Kaitlyn had put on a pot of coffee and poured two mugs before leaving.

"What's going on, Aurora?"

"What's said here can never leave this apartment."

"Of course." Chris motioned for her to take a spot at the table, pushing the vase of fragrant flowers to the side. "I assumed that's why you called me so late."

"I'm sorry. But you said…"

"No, I know." She took a sip of coffee. "Anyways."

"The desire for Percocet was overwhelming tonight. I needed a Xanax, couldn't find one and well… things progressed from there."

"I see. What brought that on?"

"A need to escape."

Her heavy, burdened eyes perked up with the comment. "I see, I see." Chris leaned closer, her gaze roving up and down. "What type of escape are we talking about here?"

Ah, yes, she got it.

"The bad kind."

"And what brought that on?"

"Feelings." It came out as a whisper, but echoed loudly in her head.

Chris leaned even closer. "What kind of feelings?"

"A couple really. But I don't know how to explain."

Chris sighed, but it sounded impatient. "Try."

She lowered her head. "There's the feeling that I'm falling for your brother."

"Yes, I'm aware. You're madly in love with Nate." Chris pulled away from her and straightened up.

"Yes, but it's also Lucas I'm having feelings for."

Chris jerked her head back. "I don't want to hear about that. You'll need to talk to someone else about *that* problem. Call Dr. Navin first thing in the morning." A strong, scolding voice emerged from the petite woman. "You called me because of the bad escape, was it?"

"In trying to deal with these thoughts, I got overwhelmed. And scared. I needed to stop the pain. I wanted to be numb from it. Give in to my weakness." She tucked her chin into her chest. "I thought if I wasn't here, I wouldn't have to constantly fight this battle anymore. I'd be free and I wouldn't have to worry about hurting anyone else."

❤ Chapter Twelve ❤

"Okay," Chris said, regaining control of her emotions, and lowering her voice. It wasn't like her to sound so angry. "Tell me why that thought happened."

"Well, if I knew that..."

"What preceded it?"

"Being overwhelmed. Like I can't do this anymore. It got to be too much. Between the therapy, the physio, the homework from the shrink, and trying to fight this fear with the PTSD, I feel as though I am losing the battle. Like I'm never going to be healed. Then when I craved the drugs, I thought 'I'm never going to get over this'. I'm always going to want them. And that scared me."

"Yes, I imagine it would. But isn't that a good thing?"

"Say what?"

"That it scared you? It means a bigger part of you is fighting the urges."

She flashed back to the pills she'd hidden between her mattress. "But the urges are still there."

"And with time, fighting them will be what drives you."

"Lucas never said anything to you, did he?"

She tilted her head and straightened herself out. "About?"

"A while ago, I took something." Unable to connect with Chris, Aurora focused on the feel of her own hands as she clasped them together. "I swear it was only Benedryl, but I took enough of them."

"Why?"

"I needed to escape. To sleep." A long pause as she exhaled. "To forget."

Chris nodded as if taking it all in. Maybe she was sorting and analyzing what it meant. Maybe she was wondering what facilities were still open so she could check her in. Whatever she was doing, the seconds ticked by painfully slow.

"What does this have to do with Lucas?" she asked.

"I gave him the rest of the pills," Aurora said.

"I see." She took a long drink from her cooling coffee, her face devoid of any emotion.

Surely, Chris had to be feeling something. She'd just admitted to a ton of things.

"And what did Lucas do with this information?"

A lump formed in the back of Aurora's throat. "He held me for quite a while and spent the night. On the couch," she added for good measure. Whatever was happening between her and Lucas, it certainly wasn't sexual, and she needed to make sure that was understood. "In the morning, we called my father, and then told Kaitlyn."

"Does Lucas stay here a lot?"

A wave of guilt crashed over Aurora as she nodded. Every night—except race night—ended the same. Despite her protests that she'd be fine, he always camped out on the couch. After awhile it just became habit. And a comfortable one at that. It soothed her nerves knowing if she needed him, he was a few steps away. Or thirty-seven. She'd counted.

"Well, that explains why mom says he's never home anymore." Chris got quiet. It drove her insane how she could sit there so still and only blink. Was it a shrink thing? "For the record, I think you're doing a great job."

So not the response she was expecting. "What?"

"You've come a long way. You should be proud. You're learning to fight the urges, and each time you resist, you'll get better and stronger. Just like that night with Lucas, and tonight. You fought the urge."

A small uncomfortable laugh escaped. "You've seen my apartment right? Trust me, I wasn't fighting the urge too well."

"Yes, I can tell a battle was brewing here." Chris glanced around the disarray. "But, Aurora, whether you believe me or not, you won that battle."

"But the thought of suicide?"

Her lips tightened, as did her expression. "Yes. That troubles me. Is this a reoccurring thought?"

"No. Dr. Navin asked me if I was happy to be alive, and that's what started the fifty things that make me happy project."

"That man loves his happiness projects." She shook her head. "When was the last time you had thoughts of suicide?"

"When I was in the hospital recovering from the accident."

"I see."

"What? What are you thinking?"

Chris put her hand up and closed her eyes.

The clock ticked loudly but Aurora figured her heartbeat was noisier.

Chris leaned into the back of the kitchen chair. "Just give me a sec."

Aurora dropped her chin to her chest and did as she was told. The wait ate at her, chewing up her insides.

"Okay, what I think we should do–"

Here it comes.

"Is cut back on everything. Can we re-schedule some of your physio visits? Maybe lessen the workload with the PTSD and the driving schedule Lucas has with you? Honestly, I think you are pushing yourself too hard. You're on the verge of snapping."

"I did snap," she corrected.

"And you're going to get worse if we don't taper off. I'm not saying to quit, because I think you still need to do what you're doing, but you need to back down. Practicing all day and night with Lucas. Therapy appointments every other day. Physio twice a week. And now you're back in university. You're just overwhelmed."

"I know."

"Taking a step back is okay."

She wished Chris was a touchy-feely person because she could really use the comfort from a tender squeeze or a full body hug.

"Call Dr. Navin tomorrow and reschedule that appointment for as soon as you can and then go weekly."

"But I don't understand how this will help."

Chris huffed, and swallowed a taste of coffee. "When I was a kid, mom put me in piano lessons with the strictest teacher on the planet. Mrs. Kensington made me do my scales at the most painful, slowest speed, and then at warp speed in time to the metronome. Over and over again. I was never allowed to play them at a regular, normal speed. However, as the time approached for testing, I got to. And you know what happened? Everything clicked into place. My scales were perfectly melodic. My songs were the right tempo. My fingers knew what to do.

"You, and your mind, you're being challenged. You did the slow version, just after your accident. Now you've been doing the speed version with Lucas. Everything is telling you it's time to slow down to a normal pace. Maybe then, everything will click into place."

She nodded and swallowed down the lump forming in her throat. "But you don't sound confident."

"Aurora, the mind is a terribly complicated thing. Nothing is textbook. I wish it were. It would make solving problems as simple as ABC. All we can do is assess your situation, see what it compares to and, really, hope for the best. If it doesn't work, we try a different route. But right now? Right now, you need a break. And Lucas needs to know that."

Her heart started to ache. How was she was supposed to cut back on her time with Lucas?

"Why are you crying?"

She recoiled in her seat as she wiped her eyes before tears could slip out. "I haven't started crying yet."

"Yeah, but you're about to. Why?"

Her vision blurred the harder she fought it. "I just have self-doubt."

"We all have that."

"Yeah. Well it occupies a lot of my thoughts. Whether or not I'm ever going to be good enough for Nate. Whether or not I'll ever get my happy ending. Whether or not I'm ever going to be healed." She folded her legs under her.

Chris leaned back on her chair. "We're all trying to heal from something. It's how you handle yourself on the journey that makes the difference."

"Yeah, well my journey sucks."

"Not really."

Aurora rolled her eyes.

"No, think about it, and hear me out on this. Every moment that happens in our life affects the one after. If you wouldn't have had your car accident, you could still be dating that Devon guy."

"Derek."

"Yes, sorry." Chris waved her away. "Anyways, you could be engaged to him, right? You might still be living in Fort Mac, and the strong possibility exists that we would never have met. But... you *did* have an accident, broke up with Derek, ended up moving here and took a job at the library where you met Nate. So I'd say your journey, albeit not the one you planned, may have been the perfect one for you."

She rested her chin on her knees. "So what now? How do I get through this?"

"I'd say you already are. You made the right decision to call me, and you resisted your urges. Sounds like you are doing okay."

"Doesn't feel like it." The desire to be held hadn't gone away, and she let her hands rest on the table, hoping Chris would reach for them.

She didn't make a move, in fact she pulled back a little more. "I know it doesn't. And I know what you're going through."

"What? You had PTSD?" The thought of knowing she had it and made it through gave her hope.

"No, not PTSD. But I've suffered through depression and suicidal thoughts." She pulled back on her sleeve and flipped her palm towards the ceiling.

A loud gasp echoed in the room.

"Yeah, mine were more than thoughts."

"Oh my god, I'm so sorry." She couldn't focus on anything else but the scar. It was about one and a half to two inches long right across the wrist. Words escaped her. "When?"

"A few months after Dad died. It was really hard to watch him suffer so much, especially right at the end. I was finishing up my degree and everything was going south. Faster than I could control."

"I'm so sorry."

"I understand the feelings you're experiencing. Believe me. And I know you'll get through them. I never called for help, but I'm thankful help found me in time."

She swallowed, and asked in a quiet voice, "Can I ask who found you?"

Chris focused on her. "My baby brother."

"I figured."

Somewhere deep down, she had to have known it was him. To her at least, it explained why he was so compassionate and empathetic.

"If you're feeling overwhelmed again, I have no issue whatsoever in you calling me. Okay? I'm here to help you."

She nodded, still thinking about Lucas.

Poor kid.

"Thank you."

Chris stood and put her mug in the sink. "Are you feeling better or worse?"

A quick internal check of her emotions and physical sensations, nothing out of the ordinary. "I'm okay."

"What do you need to get through the night?"

"A Xanax would be great." She eyed Chris with hope and a weak smile. "But I don't need it."

"Kaitlyn's coming back?"

"Yes, as soon as I text her. She's probably in the parking lot, pacing or something."

"Text her. I'll stay until she arrives." Chris placed her hand on her arm, totally catching her off guard. "But I won't give you the Xanax. I think you'll be okay."

She sighed, but Chris was probably right. She'd get what she truly craved—physical contact—from her best friend.

Kaitlyn knocked on the door within seconds of being texted. Had she paced in the hallway? "Hey, you doing okay?"

Aurora closed the door after Chris said good night. "I'm better now, thanks."

Kaitlyn threw her arms around her, giving her what she needed. Like an affectionate big sister, she smoothed her hair down in comforting passes.

"Anything I can do?"

"Nah." She pulled out of the hug. "But I wanted to say sorry. For before."

Kaitlyn stepped back and tugged on her sleeves. "For what?"

Her arms fell to the side. "For my behaviour. For not leaning on you the way a best friend should. For not being able to tell you what was going through my mind."

"Well, I won't lie. It stings a bit that you confide so much in Lucas and lean on him more, especially since I knew you first."

Aurora opened her mouth. She wanted to tell Kaitlyn that there were reasons to depend on Lucas, so many reasons, and yet, none of them seemed important at the moment.

Kaitlyn raised a hand. "Before you speak and say something you may end up regretting…" A pained smile stretched her thin lips. "I get it. I don't like it, but I get it."

She stepped forward a bit.

Kaitlyn waggled a finger between them. "You and I? We're best friends, but we're a different form of best friends than you and Lucas. Don't get me wrong, we get along great and share lots, but you two? You're on a whole other level. I don't understand the connection you have and that's what hurts."

"Kait, I'm so sorry. I never meant to hurt you." She wanted to reach out and hold her friend, but didn't dare. Kaitlyn stood there tilting her head from side to side and rocking on her heels.

The seconds ticked by, and a gust of wind billowed the curtain beside the patio door. In the far off distance, a low rumble of thunder sounded. Aurora swallowed down a gulp of fear. She could handle it. She'd been through a storm or two or three over the summer.

Kaitlyn sighed and her body rolled forward. "I know you didn't. I feel I missed so much while I was away."

"Not so much. You did manage to find love with Tatiana."

A weak smile appeared on Kaitlyn's face. "I hope so. Skype isn't enough though. I want her here. I *need* her here."

She rubbed her friend's arm. "I know you do. A few more weeks."

"Story of our lives. Big changes are coming."

"Yes they are. And I don't know about you, but I'm looking forward to it."

"Me too."

❤ Chapter Thirteen ❤

Saturday came and went at a slow crawl. Mountains of baked goods piled up on the kitchen counter. The sweet smell of chocolate, frosting, and snickerdoodles filled the air as Aurora thought of Lucas. Had he gone to the track early? At that very moment he was probably talking to Nate. Maybe finishing a race. Was the tension between him and his mom gone for the time he was at the track? Did he sleep there or at home? She felt bad that he couldn't stay at her apartment, but she needed to catch her breath and figure things out.

She wiped the excess batter on the apron before picking up her phone. No check-in text. No missed phone call.

Damn.

She'd pushed back too hard and burned another relationship. Typing furiously, she hoped if she kept it light and casual, maybe things would be okay.

The text read: Hey… wondering how you did at the track tonight…

No response.

An hour later with the kitchen clean, the baked goods wrapped and stored in the freezer, she headed down the hall to bed. Radio silence from Lucas.

She climbed into bed and texted:

11:35 pm Hey… look… I'm sorry about freaking out last night. I want to talk to you about it, explain everything. Will you call me? I'd rather not do this over text.

11:45 pm I'm sorry you'll have to spend time at your own house instead of here. I feel as though I've kicked you out of your home, and that's not what I wanted. I just needed…

11:46 pm I needed space. I still do. I need the physical distance to work through my insecurities, to figure things out. Chris said to cut back on everything. No physio, no shrinks, no car homework. Thinks I overloaded and snapped. I did… haha. If you ask her, maybe she can explain.

11:48 pm Please understand. I still need you in my life but I need to work through a way to do it so it benefits us both instead of killing us both. Can you understand that?

11:50 pm I'm probably not making much sense. Call me. Let's talk about this.

Sunday
2:02 pm Okay… you must be really mad at me. You didn't even check-in like you normally do. Don't worry, I stayed clean. But I miss you. Sunday lunch isn't the same all alone. I made your fav in hopes you'd show up.
6:04 pm Seriously?
6:06 pm Nothing? You're killing me here.
6:07 pm This isn't like you… Are you really that upset with me?
6:12 pm How can I make it up to you? My door is open.
6:13 pm Not really, but you know what I mean.

Monday
10:25 am Dr N thinks it's a good idea for us to talk in person. Cutting out the homework and everything else, shouldn't include cutting you out too. And I don't want to. I need you.
7:35 pm I miss you. It's hard not talking to you, you know?
9:41 pm Guess you're giving me the cold shoulder eh? I deserve that.
9:43 pm I'm so sorry. Will you at least text back and tell me you're okay?

Tuesday

110

5:17 pm Okay – seriously… I get it. You're mad. Obviously. How do we move through this? I can't not have you in my life.

5:22 pm I'm going crazy… not the "drug-induced or lack of" crazy but lonely crazy. I miss you.

5:26 pm Class isn't going well. Hope its going better for you.

5:30 pm Lucas??? Is your phone lost and in the hands of a total stranger and that's why you're not at least sending me an emoji? Hello??

Wednesday

8:41 pm Well it's not like I can drive over to your house and bang on the door, begging you to talk to me. Can you imagine? Me showing up at your place in a cab? LOL. Hmmm… unless that's what you're hoping for. Would be reverse psychology or something. So how do we fix this? How do I fix this?

Thursday

11:36 am Okay here's the thing. Until you tell me to fuck off, I'm going to text you everyday. Every. Single. Day. Did you read that?

2:06 pm I had physio today. My only appt all week and my last one for a while. I overdid it and earned my 'treat' the hard way. And I'll tell you something, I fuckin loved it. It felt so good. It'd been too long. But that's it. That's all I've had. Haven't even touched the Xanax, but it's there. Haven't slept much either. I think I've managed three hours each night. I keep thinking back to Friday. And I have no words. Did I overreact? Probably. Did I have reason to think what I did? Absolutely. So now what? I don't want to lose you. You mean too much. But I don't know what to do. I need to talk to you. Lucas, please. Call me. Text me. Email me. Send a telegram if you'd like. Just let me know you're okay. Please…

Friday

3:52 pm The neighbours are giving me dirty looks bc I won't stop touching their cars. You'd better come stop me. ;)

4:15 pm What no comeback to that? LOL. That was pretty good. Homework isn't the same. I have no car to sit in. :) The videos are boring without your running commentary. You really are a good colour announcer.

4:34 pm Anywho... I've been going through Carmen's things all week and used her old stuff to work on something that I hope I'll be able to show off at the track. If you'll still take me. ;(It's no PaintNite but its me.

Saturday

11:08 am I wanted to wish you good luck. I know your last race of the season is tonight. Hope your Guardian Angel drives fast. :) Miss you.

9:56 pm Hope you did well. I was cheering from here. Did you hear me?

Sunday

10:03 am We really need to talk. This is getting ridiculous. I'll have lunch ready for 1. I think you know where I live... LOL.

10:57 am Your silence is breaking my heart.

❤ Chapter Fourteen ❤

She glanced to the clock. It was after one. Lucas didn't arrive for lunch. Slowly, she rose and took his plate to the kitchen, wrapping it up and putting it in the fridge. Her own food remained mostly untouched—she'd just pushed it around. Her head fell against the refrigerator door. Foolish she had been in hoping he'd show. What was she going to do now? Would she honestly text him every day still?

It had been over a week since they talked. She fought back bitter tears as she slid down and flopped on the floor. The whole thing had been her fault. She'd been the one to freak out, and rather than work through it then and there, pushed him away. Just like she had with Nate. She was hopeless and doomed to live a life alone.

With Lucas no longer talking with her, her epic plan had already failed. He wouldn't be driving her to the track. There would be no reconciliation with Nate. She'd lost everything. Tears streamed down, staining her cheeks. Another glance to the clock. It was quarter past.

Damn.

Her hands smeared the tears over her cheeks and into her hair.

A knock sounded from her door.

She scrambled to get off the floor, her heart pounding faster than her steps.

Another knock.

Twisting the door handle, she pulled open the door.

"Hey," she said in a broken voice.

Lucas stood there, a light scent of racing fuel mixed with cologne tickled her nose. All at once it was familiar and comforting.

She wiped her eyes, hoping he couldn't tell what she'd been doing moments before.

Feet firmly planted on the weathered carpet, he stood ramrod straight with a clenched jaw.

"You could've just come in."

"It's not my home." A hurt tone interlaced into his words. He crossed his arms over his chest and shifted weight to his left leg.

She stepped to the side and gestured for him to come in. There was a moment of hesitation and a hitch in his breathing before he crossed the threshold of the apartment.

"Thank you for coming," she said. "And for coming in. I don't need the neighbours to listen in. They already think I'm strange." The door latched into place. "Would it help if I apologized again?"

"It might."

She hung her head and stared at his feet. He hadn't removed his shoes yet, which meant he wasn't likely to stay. There had to be a way to convince him. They would never work through this if he left now with so much to say.

"I'm sorry. I was confused. And scared. And overwhelmed." Taking a chance, her gaze travelled up to his face. "I'm sorry for pushing you away."

"Was I part of your problem?" His head cocked and he thrust his hand into his jeans.

"You weren't a part of the solution."

He didn't move from his spot as he scrutinized her. There was nothing creepy or romantic about it as she suspected she knew what he was doing—searching for any physical damage. "And now? Are you better?"

"Yeah. I think so." She paused. "Mostly."

"You don't sound sure." He searched again.

A painful sigh escaped her as she leaned against the door. "It's been a helluva long week. A lonely one."

Tension built between them as the moments ticked by. They stood, frozen in silence. She had hoped him showing up would mean all was forgiven, but the longer he stood there, the faster that thought dashed away.

"Is there something you wanted from me? Why'd you ask me over?"

"I don't like how things… umm… ended last Friday. I want to talk about it."

"We *are* talking."

"Can we talk in the living room?"

It worked. He kicked off his shoes and made his way over to the sofa, but he never sat down. She followed him, inhaling a huge gulp of air she hoped contained some courage.

Lucas ran his fingers through his hair and shook out his hands. "I need to tell you something. You hurt me. Essentially, you kicked me out."

"I'm sorry," she whispered. "I know you're having problems with your mom–"

"Let me finish." His long fingers massaged his temples. "That night, I had big plans. I wanted to see if the broken up trip would work out, and along the way, I was gonna make it a fun evening. I did that *for you*. I refuse to apologize if you read more into it than there was. I had nothing but fun planned, and if you thought it was of a romantic nature, then that's *your* problem."

"I know."

His voice was dark. "If you were scared, you should've said something instead of pulling into yourself. I thought we were friends. I thought I trusted you." His voice softened. "I thought you trusted me."

"I do." One foot in front of the other, she inched her way over to him. His body still turned away from her, she stopped approaching. "Lucas, something happened that night."

Be honest with him.

"I started having these feelings…"

He scrutinized her and again gave her a full body search. "What kind of feelings?" The tone in his voice had an edge.

Well… She swallowed down her pride. "I thought I was…"

Although his expression remained stoic, his eyes changed for a fraction of a second.

The courage she had a moment ago, disappeared as she exhaled. *No point in hurting his feelings.*

"I was... completely overwhelmed. I didn't understand what I was feeling. I was scared of those feelings and everything they represented, and I needed to numb them. Fast. But I had nothing to help me. I can't tell you how exactly, but something inside me snapped."

A slow head nod. His brows furrowed, but he never took his gaze off her.

"I couldn't handle those feelings anymore. It was too much. Then I felt that it wasn't fair, and this wasn't fair to anyone else. Things went south from there. In desperation I called Chris when my thoughts turned..." Her mouth was as dry as cotton. "Dark."

Lucas moved closer, his body leaning toward her.

"After talking me down from the ledge, so to speak, a decision I wasn't in agreement with came about. I had to shut everything down before everything shut me down."

He nodded and his expression softened.

She reached out for him. "I'm sorry you were a causality in that. I needed to distance myself physically from you but only until I could sort out my feelings." Her focus went straight to his grey-blues. She had his full attention. "If it's any consolation–"

"There's no consolation, Aurora."

"Please, let *me* finish." She pulled him over to the couch. Weakness was turning her legs into wet spaghetti and she wasn't sure how much longer she'd be able to stand. "But it was impossible to shut you out, can't you see that? I couldn't do it. If you can believe it, I actually missed being around cars. I missed our training sessions. I missed... you." Her heart raced much faster than the words falling out of her mouth. A long sigh, and a quick glance to see him taking in every word. "And as much as I love you, I'm in love with Nate."

He stayed tight-lipped as he tapped his foot.

"I hope you can find it in your heart to understand what I'm saying and to forgive me."

Reddish-blond hairs went flying as he shook his head. "So much happened this week, and I wanted to share it with you. My best friend. But you turned your back to me."

"That's not true. I *never* turned away from you." Her voice rose. "I texted you. Multiple times a day. I told you to come over. I

116

apologized. You…" Anger boiled inside her, heating her up. "You…
You ignored me."

Heat fanned up in the room with their rising tempers. "You
kicked me out, what was I supposed to do? How was I supposed to react?
Was I supposed to come crawling back, begging for forgiveness over
something I didn't do?"

"No, of course not."

"Then what? Tell me, Aurora. You seem to have all the
answers."

"Well for starters, you could've responded to the fucking texts
I sent. That would've been great." She stomped around, fighting the urge
to toss a throw pillow at him. Instead, she smacked her hand onto the
patio door. "I kicked you out for that one night only."

A deep breath filled her lungs. She needed to diffuse the anger
before she snapped, and that feeling was building monstrously fast. A
sweaty palm streaked up the window. "I told you you were welcome
back here. I wanted you to come back. I wanted to talk to you. If I'd
turned my back on you, would I have asked?"

Silence filled the room.

Her forehead touched the cool of the glass door, and she
welcomed the sensation. Her voice dropped. "I apologized and admitted
I'd freaked out. I thought about you all the time. How many times do I
have to tell you I missed you? How many times do I have to say I'm
sorry?"

Turning slowly, she internally screamed at him to say something
more. Like a statue, he stood there, never moving. Her hand twitched.
She searched his face, her eyes darting back and forth between his left
and right eye. For a moment, she wished she had his ability to read
people, to sense what they were feeling. All she was getting from him
was stone cold silence. What was he thinking?

Chin to chest, she sighed as quietly as she could muster.

"Make me a promise, okay?" Strong fingers rubbed his along
his jaw line as he cleared his throat.

His voice was taut, but she nodded anyway. Was he about to say
goodbye? Dread filled her core. He leaned forward enough to make it
seem as though he was preparing to walk away.

A serious expression filled his face as he stared hard, piercing right through to her soul.

"Don't shut me out again. Ever. Not for a night. Not for an hour. Not even a minute. No matter what you're thinking. No matter what you're feeling. No matter what happens on Saturday." He slipped closer to her. "Promise me, okay? You'll never shut me out again."

She nodded, her mind flipping over his words.

"Say it."

"I promise."

"Now come here," he said, his voice smoothing out.

As she stepped closer, he wrapped her in a hug. She hugged him back, hopeful things between them would be okay again. As she replayed his promise, she pushed out of the embrace.

"What's going to happen on Saturday?"

"Nate."

A shy little smile ticked at her lips. Just six more days until she could see him. Six. More. Days.

"I have some good news for you. Lots actually." He scratched his whiskery chin. "Do you want to hear it?"

"Of course." The nearest item to her was a throw pillow, which she tossed playfully in his direction.

The air in the room changed in a heartbeat. The pea-soup thick tension, anger and dark storm clouds were gone, replaced with the sunlight and light breeze. Her heart suddenly felt lighter.

He sat beside her, but kept a noticeable distance. "Now, do I tell you in chronological order, or just the best news last?"

"Just tell me," she said.

"Okay. Well, to answer one of your texts, I did very well yesterday. I came in first in the feature which gave me enough points to end the season in first place."

"Yes!" she screamed and gave him a hug. "Oh Lucas, that's wonderful. I knew you could do it. Your first win."

"They can't call me the Chaser anymore." His whole face lit up as he launched into details about how he fought to maintain his lead. It was so close as he crossed the finish line, they joked it was a photo finish. "The win will help as far as sponsorships go. Companies are more likely to give money to winners."

"You were always a winner to me."

"Awe, thanks." A crimson colour flooded his cheeks. "Oh, and one other major thing happened. It ends well, but started terribly."

She leaned closer. "What? Tell me," she said when he settled back into his seat.

"Nate and Marissa had a fight, the night after we had our... disagreement."

Her heart did a double beat.

"Right before the second heat. And it was ugly. In fact, I was more than a little embarrassed at Nate."

"*At* Nate? Not for him?"

"Ah, no. I'll spare you the details because it was nasty. Anyways, the fight brought out their demons."

"Who? Marissa and Nate's?"

"Yep. I've never witnessed either of them drive like that. They were so aggressive to each other. Nate got DQ'd."

She shook her head, not understanding. "I don't know–"

"He got disqualified during the second heat and wasn't allowed in the feature race."

"Oh my god."

"Like I said, nasty." Lucas laughed uncomfortably. "But he finally dumped her. Thank God. During the intermission, surrounded by people, unfortunately. It was very public. I actually felt bad for Marissa."

"Yikes. And you don't even like her."

"I know, right?" He twisted in his seat. "And for the good news."

"There's good news on top of that?"

"Yeah. That night, mom stayed with Bill so Nate and I had the trailer to ourselves." He hesitated and pulled back a little. "I shouldn't tell you this, but I'm gonna. And it never leaves us."

She nodded in agreement.

"He was probably too drunk to know what he said."

Aurora recoiled and pushed deeper into her seat. She was anti-alcohol, and somewhere deep down she thought Nate rejected it too, mainly because of her. It was shocking to hear he didn't.

Lucas' hands waved all over as he spoke. "I know what you're thinking. He doesn't get drunk all the time. And he never drives drunk. I swear. Normal people drink. Evil people drink and drive."

The words soothed her a little. But it was true. Most people their age did drink. And as long as they didn't get behind a wheel, they kept everyone around them safe.

Lucas shook his head. "So, Nate doesn't know I've been helping you all summer, right? Like he really has no clue. Honestly believes I've been elsewhere." Lucas chuckled, rather proud of his evasive skills. "Anyways, in his drunken stupor, he went on and on about you two. How much he missed you. How much he'll miss racing, but how you mean more, and how he wants you to be a part of Northern Lights Racing in some capacity. He was throwing out some ideas on how to try and get you back."

"And? What's he planning?"

"Retiring again. The whole thing with Marissa, well, it added to his problems. Figures he can be rid of her and get you back at the same time. Kill two birds with one stone type of thing. Anyways, it doesn't really matter what he's planning. You'll beat him to it. By a few hours. If he remembers the really awesome idea."

Her stomach fluttered with excitement. "You think so?"

"I know so."

"That makes my night, Lucas because I made something for him." She rose and walked over to the closet, gently extracting a huge poster. Turning it toward him, she said, "I've been working on it all week. It's not Carmen's caliber of artwork, but it was the best I could do." She'd spent hours first creating it and then filling it with colour. "Do you think it's noticeable enough?"

Lucas tipped his head and studied it. "I love it and you know what? It could make a great logo. Would need *some* tweaking…"

Glee filled her as she tucked it back into its spot. She fell beside him, closer this time.

"Let me ask you something." His nose twitched. "With this hiatus you took, what do we do now? How do we manage the next five days?"

"You mean six."

"No, I mean five. On the sixth day we travel."

Shit. Five days to practice—worry—stress—freak out—or get excited. Depending on how you look at it.

"I honestly don't know. Any ideas?"

"Hmm…" He rubbed his chin in thought. "What about a round trip drive somewhere that would be roughly twenty minutes? You need to be able to handle at least a fifteen-minute drive for Saturday. It would make the drive there much easier to plan." He grabbed his phone. "What do you say to that?"

A slow nod. "Maybe." Another nod. "It should work."

"Or would it be too much?"

"I don't think so. It's only one trip, not the thirty or forty attempts of a trip in one night."

"So… Can I drive you to class tomorrow?"

❤ Chapter Fifteen ❤

Lucas

There she is.

His best friend emerged from her apartment building like a breath of fresh air. As much as she'd been anticipating this day all summer, he sure as hell hadn't. Yeah, he wanted her to succeed in her goals and he was happy he'd been there for the ride, but it all ended today. After this, she'd be riding with someone else. The one her heart belonged to.

Swallowing down a morsel of sadness and clearing his throat, he asked, "You all set?" He approached the girls.

Aurora's long, dark hair hung loosely around her delicate face, and if he didn't know better, he'd wager a guess she was wearing makeup. Her blue eyes were more radiant and sparkly than normal. But underneath it all, he knew better–she was nervous.

Her hands twitched and her confident walk was long gone. There was no reason for her to be nervous though, she'd been doing great all week with the single trip to the U in the morning and back home again.

With a shaking hand, she lifted her purse, a coat for later, and the poster.

Kaitlyn walked up behind them, draping an arm over Aurora's shoulders. "She's a nervous wreck."

"Good." He smiled. "It gives us something to focus on."

He popped the trunk and placed her things into it. Walking over to the passenger door, he motioned for her to get in.

"Good luck," Kaitlyn said, giving Aurora a quick peck on the cheek.

She whispered something inaudible. Whatever it was, it made Aurora smile and seeing it always made his day. It was gorgeous—an ear to ear grin showcasing perfectly straight teeth.

Nate was a lucky dog.

"Sure, you won't follow us?" Aurora's voice squeaked as she turned to Kaitlyn.

"As much as I'd love to see how this plays out, I can't. But call me later."

"Okay," she said.

Poor thing shook so hard she needed the stability of the passenger door to hold her up.

Kaitlyn blew a kiss and walked away.

They were back to being just them. He gave her a full once over. Sneakers, navy blue shorts, tan-coloured tank top. Her chest moved rapidly as she breathed. He skimmed up a little higher and stopped at her lips. They trembled ever so slightly, and her nose twitched, but her eyes...

Aurora's sky-blue eyes darted between him to the passenger seat and back again. Her sweet smell was intoxicating as she stood beside him, shaking out her limbs and cocking her neck.

Not gonna sweat this, need to keep everything calm and relaxed.

He leaned casually against the car. "Whenever you're ready. We have lots of time."

She huffed and puffed, took a deep breath and fell in against the seat.

"All good?" Lucas asked.

When she gave him a nod, he closed the door and rushed to his side. He slipped behind the wheel and slid on his Ray-Bans, waiting to start the car until she gave him the signal. Slowly, she poked up her thumb from her fist.

"Alrighty." The car rumbled to life beneath them and he put it in reverse, easing it out nice and slow. "First stop, Tim Hortons."

As much as he'd love to talk with her, he knew better. This week—especially with the longer trips—she'd developed a coping mechanism that hadn't been there as strong before her time off. Now, she either hummed or rapidly tapped out some sick Morse code signals on her lap. Either way, she usually stayed in her zone. Not a great travel companion per se, but at least they were going places. He'd have to remember to tell this to Nate for the ride home.

The first part of the trip passed much quicker than anticipated as there was no traffic and he made all the lights but two. She'd instinctively reached for his hand during the first leg, and he held it with fervor. Once, not too long ago, she'd told him it was a grounding mechanism. He liked that. It made him feel useful. Something else he'd have to mention to Nate.

Dammit, that guy had all the luck. He has the better race car, and the new company–Northern Lights Racing–launched last night. He and Nate were up until the wee hours working on Facebook and Twitter accounts, following the right people, places and groups. Nate had made him full partner in the hopes that by next spring, Lucas would be his star racer. His overall season winning should help. With the upcoming banquet, there'd be a chance to meet and acquire new sponsorships, as next season he'd be racing under his brother's banner. It made him nervous and excited at the same time.

He turned his head and admired the beautiful girl in his passenger seat. Still tapping out Morse code with her right hand, her face appeared peaceful and relaxed. Deep into the zone and doing very well. If she kept this up, the trip should be a breeze, which was good.

He'd made the drive to the track so many times he was sure he could do it in his sleep, his last trip down he'd marked out stops. Places to rest, get a drink, and emergency stops. Just in case. He had it all planned out.

Thankfully, the first leg was drama free as he rolled into the parking lot of their first destination, Tim Horton's—his favourite—and stopped.

He rushed to open her door, extending his hand to her. "You did great."

"Thanks," she said, holding his hand tightly as he pulled her onto her feet.

He kept an eye on her, watching for signs of too much stress. So far, nothing out of the ordinary. Always one to plan for the what ifs, a couple Xanax were packed for emergency use, compliments of Chris.

They were hidden safely in the pocket of his jeans. She had stressed—repeatedly, as if he were a supreme idiot, and not Aurora's best friend—how important it was to allow her to call the shots and to read her emotions. A skill he already possessed in spades. One of the major reasons he was transferring to psych next term. It didn't matter what his Mom said. He just felt drawn to that career path. Yeah, the money was an issue, a huge one, but he'd figure it out one way or another. That's why they invented student loans.

The Timmy's was packed, and it took nearly fifteen minutes for them to wait in line and order. With a cold drink for him and a bottle of water for her, they pushed through the crowds and rested outside. Cars lined the drive-thru, inching their way to the front. Didn't matter what time of the day he drove past here—there was always a line up.

He slurped on the Ice Capp she bought him, loving the way it cooled him down. The heat rose all around him, and the forecast said it would be a great night, although there was a small chance of storms. Hopefully those waited until they'd left the track.

"Want a sip?" he asked, tipping the drink in her direction.

Silently, she shook her head, covering her face against the rays of sunlight.

Just as well. Empty tummy means a lesser chance of throwing up.

The car had just been detailed so he could sell it and use the extra cash for school. The resale value would sink like a lead weight with the stench of vomit. Rumor has it *that* smell never comes out.

"I'm ready for more. Let's continue." Her sweet voice broke him out of his wandering thoughts. Aurora shook out her hands as she paced.

"Alrighty then," he said, checking his watch. Ahead of schedule. He'd budgeted a thirty-minute break, and she was raring to go within twenty.

Well done.

He opened the door and patiently waited for her to make the first move. God, Nate would be so impressed with her, and just as proud as Lucas was. The new adventure to and from university was a fifteen-minute, twice a day success. Come Monday morning, Nate would be driving her. At least that's what Lucas assumed. But only if she wanted him to. Maybe she wouldn't be comfortable with Nate? Was it wrong to hope that?

The gentlest arm pat touched him, and he focused back on her. She folded back into the seat, colour draining as she went.

Lucas waited for the thumbs up. It had been a while since they'd done back-to-back trips. The best part, aside from her actually conquering her fears, was the closeness afterwards. If she felt she'd failed, she snuggled into his arms. If she made it without a blackout or a stomach dumping, she jumped into his arms. Total win-win for him.

He was about to ask if she was okay, when he saw her signal. "Great. We'll stop in Leduc and watch the airplanes, okay?"

"That works."

They had lots of time still, something he made sure to keep in excess. Two more stops to go, and she'd likely need a longer rest at the next one. If traffic was good, it should take about twenty minutes. He needed to drive through town, rather than around it. He had no issue stopping on the side of the highway to watch the planes, but that really wasn't the best spot for Aurora. She deserved some place safer. The Visitor Information Center in town was the ideal location. Plus, there were benches and picnic tables, with lots of space to walk and stretch.

Heart-pounding, he opened Google maps and cheered *woot-woot* when he saw nothing but green lines–free-flowing traffic. Relief filled him.

On the northern edge of Leduc, Aurora's hums changed in pitch. *This isn't good.*

A second later, she stopped humming all together. *Shit.*

Her breathing increased, and her normal rhythmic tapping ceased. Instead, she pushed her hands harshly into her thighs. *No... No...*

His heart hammered in his ears and dread pooled in his lap. She was on edge and very close to going over.

"Aurora?"

Don't black out. Don't black out.

He gripped the steering wheel with more strength than was necessary.

Her breaths grew shallower and shallower. "It's sneaking in. It's sneaking in." Her fists were clenched as tight as her eyes.

"Okay," he said, trying to remain calm.

Distract. Distract. Distract.

"I want you to think of Nate. Right now." Chris mentioned how he needed to be firm in his tone, but he was terrified of scaring her further. He swallowed and spoke with authority. "Tell me what you see."

White-knuckling, he turned onto the service road. They were so close now. Could he keep her focused on Nate for long enough to get them to stop number two?

"I see Momma beside me." She inhaled.

Oh shit. Yellow light.

With his attention focused on her, he hadn't been watching the lights and planning accordingly. It was either gun it through or come to a full stop.

Shit!

Pedal to the floor, he increased the speed and drove through. It turned red half-way into the intersection.

Keep her focused.

"Where's Nate?"

"He's not there."

Dammit, another red light.

He glanced all around. Cars in every direction. A strip mall ahead, not ideal, but at this point in time, it's better than having her breakdown in the middle of 50th Street.

Should I still chance the VIC? It's only a kilometer away.

Trying to keep the panic from his voice, he swallowed down his fear and said, "Look harder, do you see him? Is he in the background somewhere?"

From the corner of his eye, she shrunk further into the seat. "It's too dark."

No... oh God, she's about to go under.

He squeezed the steering wheel in anger. Not angry with her, just mad that traffic wasn't moving fast enough.

Doesn't anyone know what's going on in here?

He breathed out in a huff. In trying to keep her collected, and himself to a small degree, he rested his hand over hers. Geez, it was cold. Like ice. "Keep looking. I'm sure he's there. Take a few more steps."

Relief settled over him as a smile broke out and she said, "I found him."

"What's he doing?"

Finally! The parking lot was ahead, but he needed to wait for the car in front of him to inch through the intersection first.

Move it, buddy.

"He's looking at me, but he's smiling and seems very happy."

Great.

Turning the car into the parking lot, he parked in the first available spot. Aurora continued her focus on whatever image played out in her head, so he jumped out and raced over to her door. Wiping away a bead of sweat and throwing out the tinge of fear he had, he opened her door.

"I figured you needed some air," he said, hoping to sound casual.

"I thank you for that." She escaped the confines of the car and wasted no time stepping over to a picnic table. Leaning against the edge, she stretched out. "One more leg and we'll be there."

A loud sigh blew from her lungs and her hands shook off their restless energy.

It was easy to empathize her plight.

"And you're doing great." He really couldn't be more proud of her.

"I was worried there for a bit."

"I gathered." Lucas stretched out beside her.

With each inhale of air, her colour started to return. He needed to stay here longer than planned as he didn't think he'd lose her on *that* trip. Figured if it was going to happen, it would be on the next leg. He stood and paced off his nervousness, hoping she didn't notice.

Her eyes were closed and turned up to the sun so he was safe. Although he knew all about her mom, after many middle of the night conversations, it always put her at ease to ask about her. He felt she needed to be put at ease now. He knew he certainly did. "What was she like? Your mom, I mean."

Her eyes opened, and instantly connected with him. "Beautiful, wonderful, smart. Kind-hearted, but firm. She'd be the first to scold us, and the first to tell us how proud she was." She stretched out her arms above her head. "What about you? What was your dad like?"

Discussing it always made him uncomfortable, so Lucas just shrugged. First it was two years of tests, illnesses, chemo treatments until he became bedridden for the final two weeks. Death was almost easier to deal with as the uncertainty of how each day would unfold was gone. For a while, at least there was peace. Then his mom had a breakdown and Nate dropped out of racing, unable to be at the track without his—their—dad. And Chris? Well, she had been a completely different issue.

"I don't remember much anymore, just little things really. The way he adored my mom and was always such a gentleman." Even in those final days, his dad exuded kindness.

"A trait he passed on well to his boys."

His cheeks heated, and it spread right over his face. "Thanks. We try to keep him smiling... wherever he is." He searched the sky, wondering if he was watching over them.

Behind them lay the highway. The roar of passing cars soothed him. One of his favourites sounds.

Aurora kept glancing nervously in the same direction. "Is this going to work out? Our big plan?"

He stepped closer to her and sat down. "It has to. He wasn't happy with her the way he was with you."

"Maybe." She shrugged.

"C'mon." He hopped off the table and held out his hand. "Let's walk and check out the area."

Hand in hand, they strolled around the building, stopping as a plane thundered overhead. It touched down on the other side of the highway.

Aurora dropped onto the grass and stretched out.

"What are you doing?"

"Watching the planes, silly. It's a different perspective like this."

He stood over her for a moment, taking in the beauty laying on the green grass. Yeah, this stop was the perfect stop. Here, behind the building, she was away from the car and the parking lot. She was grounding herself–literally–as she wiggled on the grass, feet flat, knees bent, with her hands rested gently on her stomach. Not wanting to pass up what would probably be his last chance to be with her, he stretched out beside her.

Tonight, he'd planned on following her back home, but then what? It would be super weird to follow them up, wouldn't it? Would he still be welcome at the apartment after tonight? How often would Nate be staying there? That was something he hadn't thought all the way through. What now? For a moment, his heart ached.

Plane after plane soared overhead. Each time, she inhaled a large gasp of air which made him laugh. Seriously, she was too cute. But it was time to go. If they were to make it to the track on time, it would be best to break up this moment and power on. Climbing to his feet, he dusted down his legs.

Aurora rose and ran her hands over his shoulders. "Grass." She firmly swatted him. "Well, shall we go? My destiny awaits."

He snickered. "Yeah, and he doesn't know you're coming. This'll be so awesome."

He couldn't wait to see Nate's reaction. When Nate had been with Aurora, he was a changed man–a guy with a purpose it seemed. With that hoe-bag, he was miserable and surly, and a total pain-in-the-ass to be around. He couldn't wait to have the happy Nate return, especially with the new business underway.

Last night the guys had a good talk and Nate had shared with him other plans for getting back together. It was so hard to pretend to be in the dark about Aurora, especially since Nate kept asking rhetorical questions that he actually had the answers to. After tonight, things were going to be different. Easier. And he looked forward to that. Sort of.

Buckled in and ready to go, Lucas asked, "Are you sure you're ready? This is the longest leg."

I hope the break was a true break and she'll handle this leg with no issues.

Mentally, he flipped through the emergency places he could safely stop at. He'd marked out five, all after the ten-minute point in the leg. Would he need any?

"I think I can handle it. I've made it this far."

"Yes, you have," he said, putting the car into gear.

If you can do it, I can too.

He tapped his finger against the wheel to rid himself of nervous energy. A flash of light bounced off his racing flag key-chain.

'Never Drive Faster than Your Guardian Angel Can Fly'

He gave a quick glance to his right.

She had clenched up again, as if in doing so, it would keep out the memories, flashbacks and trauma. Her legs pulled close against the seat, her arms rigid, her hands in tight little fists.

Carmen, Angelina, if you're following us, please watch over Aurora. Keep her safe. Keep her calm. She's worked too hard to have this all slip away.

She clearly needed a distraction, just as much as he did. It was enough to make sure *he* arrived safe and sound. It was extra hard—mentally and emotionally—to make sure Aurora did the same.

"Music?"

"Yeah, sure. Something to focus on." Her breathing moved from deep to shallow in a few heartbeats. Her head rolled forward.

Geezus—we're not even out of town yet. C'mon!

The Ice Capp soured in his stomach.

He peeked to the overhead storage for music. Nothing much in there she'd want to listen to. She liked the top forty crap on the radio. Not real music in his opinion.

There it is.

One of his favourites. Who knows, maybe something completely different would be a welcome distraction? He'd know if it curled her toes or relaxed her to the core.

He fiddled and inserted the CD. When it kicked in, the most amazing symphony surrounded them. The recording was crystal clear. It was like being right in Carnegie Hall, sitting in the fourth row. The string section played with gusto while the brass instruments trumpeted along. Deep in the back, if you listened hard enough, the melodic harmony from a harp tantalized the eardrums. A gorgeous sultry singer—Guilia Bianchi—one he'd spent many nights watching on YouTube, began singing. He hoped it worked on her, like it did on him. Often, especially after a crazy night of racing, he'd find the music to take him away and soothe his rattled nerves.

She laughed slightly. "What is this?"

"Italian opera." He turned it up a notch. "I have no idea what she's singing about, but I make up my own ideas based on the pitch and tone of her voice."

A smile built from his core. Each glance in her direction, he relaxed as much as she did. The first to unwind were her fists, and then her arms. With that, his grip slackened and the sour build-up diminished. As the diva pierced his heart with her universal outpouring of love, he noticed Aurora's body posture sink into the seat. It worked on her, just like he hoped.

It made the car ride seem much shorter than it was. The car crunched over the gravel parking lot where he stopped near the main gate and killed the ignition. He stroked the top of her hand. "We're here."

"What? We're here?"

Pride radiated out of him, but it was mirrored back onto him.

Her eyes grew wide as she took in her surroundings. "Oh my god, I did it. I really fucking did it."

She unlatched herself and jumped out of the vehicle, racing over to him before he could step out. Lunging into his arms, she squeezed him tight. "Thank you, Lucas."

He wrapped his arms around her. Part one of the big plan had been a complete success.

"My pleasure." He set her on the ground. "Thank you for listening to opera with me. No one likes opera."

"Nate does."

"Except him. Mom hates it."

"Really? I need to listen to it more, it was fascinating."

He beamed. "You go in through there." A small crowd gathered around the entrance. "Sit up near the announcer's booth and I'll come back after I go say hi to the family."

"You won't say anything, right?"

A chuckle escaped him. "Not a word, promise. They know I'm not racing tonight, obviously," he cracked a grin. "But it would be weird if I didn't at least drop in and say hi."

Her smiled melted his heart. Needing a distraction, he popped open the trunk.

"Your things." He grabbed her bag. A small white envelope bearing his name slipped from the side pocket. He picked it up, holding the thick packet in his hands.

"For you. For later." Her eyes danced between him and the main entrance.

"Go," he said, latching the trunk shut, the envelope tight between his fingers.

With a last glance towards the car, she held her gear and turned away from him. While waiting for her to walk through the main gates, he debated opening the small package. Sighing, he tucked it into the overhead storage and drove into the driver's lot. Game face on, he went to meet up with his family.

❤ Chapter Sixteen ❤

Lucas sauntered into the pit, trying hard to keep his emotions in check, but it was so damn hard knowing she sat a few hundred feet away. It had been easy to locate her in the stands as she sat where he instructed, soaking up the last of the summer rays. As much as she discussed going into the pit with him right at the beginning, he'd managed to talk her out of it. It was too hard on him, on everyone really, having her in the pit, so up close and personal with the cars. At least it had been last time she was there. For now, where she sat, it gave her distance. Hopefully she wouldn't puke like she did last time.

Nate stood by his car twenty feet in front of him, wiping the windows and readying himself for what he believed was his last race. If he only knew. A spring in his step, he hopped closer to his big brother, and stole a glance into the crowd. Turning back to Nate, he froze in his tracks.

That hoe-bag. Marissa approached and placed her whorish hand on Nate's arm. Panic flooded through him.

They'd better not be getting back together.

He inched towards his brother while repeatedly checking on Aurora in the stands.

"Tell your dad thanks for all the deals on the wheels," Nate said.

"Tell him yourself." She laughed, but it was shrill, like nails on a chalkboard. "He'll be here tomorrow."

"I won't be. Tonight's my last race."

"Because of me?"

Dream on, you hoe-bag. He wants someone else. Someone better. Someone awesome.

"My heart's no longer in it." Nate slammed a drawer on the toolbox shut, startling him.

Lucas didn't like the nasty feelings she created within him. After that gong show of a dinner, he actually went for a jog, and he's never done that. How in hell did Nate manage to stay with her for as long as he did? Was it the sex? He shuddered and searched to the grandstand, wondering if Aurora could see this exchange going on. He wished she were close enough to read.

Marissa lessened the distance between her and Nate. "Well, I'm sorry to hear that but this won't be the last time we'll see each other."

She stood there silently as if waiting for him to say more. He never did, and she ambled away.

Lucas tapped his brother on the shoulder.

Nate turned towards him, sadness descending on his face.

"Why so sad?"

Nate sighed. "It's over."

"Thank God." He searched the nearby groups of people, relieved the hoe-bag wasn't around. Returning to Nate, he said, "Oh, you mean about tonight."

Nate cocked an eyebrow at him.

"You know what I think you should do?"

Nate shook his head. The retirement weighed on him, adding years to his expression.

Lucas felt sorry for him.

How to keep his heart in tonight's race? Because it's not over, it just seems that way.

The lightbulb went off. "I think you should go out tonight and race for these people. Give them their monies worth and go out a winner. Make that ridiculous incident from two weeks ago seem like it never happened."

He gave his big brother a squeeze.

God, that was a friggin' embarrassment.

"Go out there and show the people what they want to see. Some hard core racing." With a gentle kick to the car, he continued, "Give 'em hell, but not too much, you just got the beast back together."

A secret he'd kept from Aurora. She'd be devastated if she knew Nate had been in a *minor* pileup last weekend.

"Have you seen Mom? I wanted to let her know I'm going up to watch from the stands."

"Really?" Nate threw a towel on top the toolbox. "Kind of odd."

"Nah. You don't need me down here tonight. The beast is perfect. You're gonna kick ass and tonight will be a night you won't soon forget." Pride radiated from him.

Nate slumped against his car. "You're telling me."

He patted him on the arm. "I can promise you, it'll be great. I'm off to find Mom."

By the time the moon rose, Nate's class of cars were readying. Aurora twisted in her seat, drumming her fingers on her lap.

"You're doing great." Lucas wrapped an arm over her shoulders. "You've managed fantastically so far. You should be proud of yourself." He gave her a comforting squeeze and caught himself when he lingered a bit too long. Tonight was for her. For Nate. "Don't watch if you don't want to."

"I think it's important that I do," she said.

It took amazing restraint on his part to not lean back and simply stare at her. Her concern made her nail picking endearing. The way she nibbled on her bottom lip made her cute. The way she fought her demons to make it to the track and win the man of her dreams was what made her beautiful.

Nate's a lucky guy.

Nate drove well. Fantastically well. At this rate, he really would go out a winner. Baring an incident like the one a couple of weeks ago, a podium spot would be his.

"I thought you said Nate's heart wasn't in it?" She nudged Lucas, a nervous smile edged the corners of her lips.

"Maybe he changed his mind for his final race. You know, go out a winner and all?"

Leaning back, he was torn between watching the race and watching her. Each lap, she inched forward, threatening to fall off if the race lasted much longer. Her focus seemed to glued to the board, but shifted slowly onto the cars; her head following the circular movement of the track.

Marissa clipped the second place holder, causing her to spin out, and narrowly avoided the racer.

Aurora gasped, and he rested his hand on hers. It was cool to the touch, and she trembled beneath his grasp.

The caution flag dropped, and the race slowed to a crawl.

He snuggled closer. "It's all good. Remember, we watched all those videos?"

"Uh huh," she said, unable to remove her focus off Nate's car.

His heart skipped a beat. Not for any reason other than he knew the end was near. His time with Aurora finished. The race would be over in seven short laps. A podium spot was guaranteed for Nate. Along with the trophy, Aurora would be his too. Too bad that after the race, he'd go back to just being the little brother.

The flag dropped green and the final seven laps were exactly what Lucas hoped to see. Nate fought to hold onto the lead, and it had the fans cheering and hollering.

It was difficult to not watch the race. His focus shifted between the track and Aurora. Between her gasps and twitches, the race was impossible to watch. Yet there was some seriously excellent racing going on that he needed to watch for himself. He'd been witness to Marissa's aggressive driving firsthand, but seeing it from the stands was nerve-wracking. The distance between cars impossibly close. Truly, the fans were going to be pleased with this fantastic night of racing.

The white flag flew—the final lap—and Aurora sat on the edge of her seat. He reached out and gently pulled her back as she blocked his view. Nate just had to hang onto first for four more turns. Three turns. Two turns. Final turn.

Aurora screamed with untold joy as Nate crossed the line, the checkered flag his.

"Let's go down," he said, nodding toward the crash fence where the top three drivers parked.

They raced down the grandstand and stood at the fence. He pushed her closer to Nate and stepped back. Her nervousness obvious as she unrolled her poster with shaking hands and placed it up against the metal.

In the background, the announcer babbled on with the third and second place winners but Lucas only had eyes for Aurora, who only had eyes for his big brother. Nate sat on the edge of his car window, his helmet gently placed on the roof, lest he scratch it. He wasn't focused on the crowds, but rather down the line toward Marissa.

You're looking in the wrong direction, butthead.

As the announcer walked over to Nate, he hopped out of his car. Beside him, Aurora lifted the poster higher against the chain-link fence. She smiled with nervous tension above it. His heart hammered in his ears, drowning out the gathering crowd.

The announcer asked, "So how was the race for you?"

Nate held the mic. "It was good. I was a little nervous that Marissa would take me out at one point."

He laughed as he pointed toward her, giving her a friendly wave.

Way to be cool, ass.

"But it's all good. It's the spirit of the game, right?" Continuing on, he thanked his competitors for making the sport fun, and his sponsors for making it possible.

The announcer handed him the first place trophy.

Next to him, Aurora took a deep breath. Lucas ran his hand over her back.

Nate held his prize, and words failed to escape him.

LOOK OVER HERE!

His eyes darted between Nate and Aurora.

"Thank you," Nate said after the announcer gave him a small nudge. "I have an announcement to make, and tonight's win makes it even harder."

The trophy twisted in his hands.

"Tonight's race is my–" As he glanced around the stands, he stopped searching when he saw her. He stepped forward, read the poster and roved his eyes upwards. "What the hell?" He was unaware of the mic in his hand, and the fact that it was still broadcasting. The air was electric. "Aurora?"

Him calling her name was like an arrow shot through Lucas' heart.

"Seriously?" Nate's voice held shock and untold joy.

Lucas put his hand on her shoulder, and whispered, "Go to him."

138

The crowd beside her stepped back. He pushed her towards the open gate where the guard with the goofy grin stood.

Nate met her at the wall. "You're here. You're really here."

She nodded and stepped over to the edge of the wall.

"How?"

"Lots and lots of practicing."

A smile larger than Lucas had seen in recent weeks lit up his brother's face. Noticing the mic in his hand, Nate passed it to the announcer behind him and returned his focus to her. "But–"

"I did it for you *and* me."

Lucas followed behind her. When she turned and saw him, his heart beat with a little less strength. She was beyond beautiful, and he'd remember this—the way she glanced at him, hair billowing in the gentle breeze, radiating with untold pride and joy. And love. For someone else.

"He helped me. We wanted it to be a surprise."

Nate looked from Aurora to him and back to her again. "I… I'm totally surprised."

"Please don't retire. I know how much this sport means to you." Her voice cracked like his heart. "You said you'd never give up on me, so here I am today." She pulled a necklace out from under her shirt. "Love, hope and faith, right?"

His family—Mom, Chris, and Max, Chris' boyfriend—all sprinted out from the pit onto the track. Each wearing a smile the size of Ontario.

Nate lifted her onto the asphalt, and in doing so, turned her so Lucas could see her face and how happy she was to be in Nate's arms.

Her voice echoed throughout the track as the announcer hadn't yet stepped away. "You had faith in me that I'd overcome my fear, and I'm working on it because I'm standing here before you. Drug free, I may add."

If Lucas was a light, his own pride would've lit up the track.

"The racing is part of who you are. I was a fool to say your hobby and my fear don't belong together because it's *what* brought us together. You told me you loved me, and with all my heart I am so in love with you, and I have faith that we can be together again. Can you ever forgive–"

Lucas turned away as Nate kissed Aurora. His heart splintering the longer the crowd roared. He grabbed the heap of items she left at the base of the fence and rolled up the poster. Once he had everything, he went back over to the guard who let him through and he joined his family on the track.

"I owe you a huge apology, Aurora," his mom said as they walked into the pit. "You've come so far since Nate's accident. I'm taking back what I said. You are good for Nate and I'm so glad everything worked out the way you hoped."

He was thrilled she'd finally accepted Aurora. It had been a tough sell convincing her Aurora had changed, but he did his part. He helped her succeed with her goal of overcoming her fears. He helped her get the man of her dreams. Like a phoenix he watched her rise from the ashes and spread her wings. He'd be forever grateful for the trust she put in him, and the endless time they spent together, but she belonged to someone else, and he had to let her go.

by H.M. Shander

Aurora's List of 50 Things

1. Nate
2. Lucas
3. Kaitlyn
4. baking
5. music
6. sex
7. *waves on a beach*
8. *girls nite*
9. Percocet
10. xanax
11. clean clothes
12. an apartment to live in
13. food in my fridge
14. access to health care
15. Daddy's insurance
16. a warm bed to sleep in
17. hot running water
18. access to education
19. **enough milk for cereal**
20. *barista spelling your name right*
21. *turkey/cheese/mayo/cucumber*
22. *freshly brushed teeth*
23. the smell of coffee
24. a perfect truffle
25. warmth of a blanket
26. birds chirping
27. a rainbow
28. a sunset over the river
29. a belly laugh
30. trust in a friendship
31. a long walk under the stars
32. surprise get togethers
33. a picnic for two
34. green jelly beans
35. a patient nurse
36. conversations with Daddy
37. playing on my phone
38. Once Upon A Time
39. spare batteries
40. sparkly nail polish
41. Chris and her help
42. the neighbour with tea
43. apple lemon twist tea
44. a working pen
45. my daily thank you
46. the shooting star I wished on
47. my pink lace bra & panties set
48. waterproof mascara
49. hugs from Lucas
50. sweet kisses from Nate

Dear Reader

I hope you enjoyed *That Summer* as much as I enjoyed writing it. I really love Aurora and Lucas, and the wonderful, deep friendship between them. Is it more than that? Or is it just friendship? Only I know for sure. Things are about to get a giant shake up with the third novel, coming in later 2017, so watch for that, as life hasn't quieted down for the MacIntyres nor the Johnsons.

As an author, it makes my day when someone shares their thoughts, and gives me feedback on the characters you've invested your time with. It's because of early feedback on *Duly Noted* that *That Summer* has come alive. Share with me what you liked, what you loved, or even what you hated. I'd love to hear from you. Are you #TeamNate or #TeamLucas?

Contact me via email (hmshander@gmail.com) or via my website (www.hmshander.com).

Finally, I need to ask you a favour. If you are so inclined, I'd love a review or a rating of *That Summer*. Loved it or hated it, I will enjoy your comments.

As I'm sure you can tell from my books, reviews are tough to come by. As a reader, you have the power to make or break a book. If you have the time, please leave a rating/reviews on my Goodreads page. All posted reviews on the retailer site, or on Goodreads, will give you early access to the next novel. Something to keep in mind.

I try my very best to reward my readers, since it's because of you, I continue to write.

Thank you so much for spending time with me.
Yours,
H.M. Shander

Other Books by H.M. Shander

Run Away Charlotte

Charlotte trusts only three people in her life - those who loved her through her darkest points.
When she meets Andrew, she slowly starts opening up to him as he courts her. Together, they learn about love and fall into it together.
However, a summer apart tests their relationship.
Upon his return home, Charlotte questions everything she's put her heart into, challenging what her heart needs verses what her mind says she deserves.

Ask Me Again

Thirteen years in an unhappy marriage cause Charlotte to feel alone and unloved.
When her first true love comes back into her life via a freak accident, she finds herself fighting against the feelings he brings out in her.
He represents safety and passion. Around him, she can be herself.
When her life falls apart, she has a choice to make once again.
And this time, her life depends on it.

Duly Noted

PTSD rules Aurora's life, keeping her from being anything more than a broken, damaged, lonely nineteen-year-old.
Until she meets charming, dashing Nate.
He wants to help and wants her to be part of his world. As he guides her away from her fears, he starts healing her heart.
However, PTSD isn't finished with Aurora yet. In order to overcome her greatest fear, she'll need to face it head on.

Acknowledgements

Thank you firstly (as always) to my family – to Hubs, Bear and Buddy, and my parents. Your unending support means the world to me. You are my biggest cheerleaders, and for that I will be eternally grateful. I may get a raised eyebrow or two when you've read what I've written, but I know you'll love it regardless.

To my Critique Partner Anya – A million thank yous and Starbucks across the miles will never be enough to repay you for your thoughts, your honesty, your critiques, your unending support *and* your friendship. I could not stand where I am without your help and dedication. You truly have a gift with words. I am forever thankful to know you.

To my beta readers – ladies your thoughts and objections to the MS were helpful in shaping it up and turning into the story it is now. I appreciate all your advice and feedback. This is why I trust you as my betas. You rock.

To my cover designer Melissa – As soon as I saw the cover, it was all I could picture as being *the* cover. Your tweaks and adjustments made it perfect. I can't see *That Summer* in any other form. Thank you for making the tiny little tweaks over the Christmas break. I appreciate it.

To my editor Natasha – Thank you for all the work you put into my manuscript, and all the little extras you did as well. Thank you for getting it done ahead of schedule despite your newborn and moving.

To KBR – words are never enough. You may not know it, but I took in every word TK shared with me about racing from sway bars to engines to everything in between. If I had a question, he answered it. His loss to his family and friends is immeasurable, and I personally will miss our late-night chats. Know he loved you dearly and was so proud of his family. I'll see you out at the track—many times—and probably in between.

If I missed you, it certainly wasn't intentional. I know I couldn't be where I am without the help of so many others. Thank you! And thank you for reading and making it all the way to the end. You all rock.

About the Author

H.M. Shander knows four languages—English, French, Sarcasm and ASL—and speaks two of them exceptionally well. Any guesses which two? She lives in the most beautiful city in Canada-Edmonton, AB, a big city with a small-town feel, where all her family live within a twenty-minute drive. As much as she'd love the beach under a blanket of stars, this is her home.

A big-time coffee addict, she prefers to start her day with a mug before attending to anything pressing. When she gave it up for Lent, totally felt Aurora's dependency and struggle through withdrawal, albeit on a much smaller scale. The Sunday morning coffees were a Godsend. She is a self-proclaimed nerd (and friends/family will back this up), reveling in all things science, however likes to be creative when there's time. Right brain, left brain? Both.

Did you know she once wanted to be a "Happy Clown" as she enjoys making people smile, but she's beyond terrified of scary clowns. How ever many different jobs she's worked, her favourite has been working as a birth doula and librarian, in addition to being an author and writing romances. Because, let's be honest, who doesn't love falling in love?

Five things she loves, in no particular order; The Colour Blue, The Smell of Coconut & Shea Butter, Star Wars, The Ocean, and Chocolate

You can follow her on Facebook, Twitter and Goodreads. She also has a blog (hmshander.blogspot.ca) she writes on from time to time.

Thanks for reading– all the way to the very end.

Made in the USA
Charleston, SC
01 March 2017